Cold Midnight
in Vieux Québec

Cold Midnight
in Vieux Québec

A Tom Austen Mystery

by
Eric Wilson

HarperCollins*Publishers*Ltd

The author describes many real places and events in this book, but the story and the characters come entirely from his imagination.

First published in 1989
by Harper and Collins Publishers Ltd.

This reprint published by
HarperCollins*PublishersLtd*
Hazelton Lanes
55 Avenue Road, Suite 2900
Toronto, Ontario M5R 3L2

Canadian Cataloguing in Publication Data

Wilson, Eric
    Cold midnight in vieux Québec

(A Tom Austen mystery)

ISBN 0-00-223495-5 (bound). - ISBN 0-00-617969-X (pbk.)
I. Title. II. Series: Wilson, Eric. A Tom Austen mystery.

PS8595.I583C65 1989   jC813' .54 C89-094844-5
PZ7.W5Co 1989

90 91 92 93 OFF 10 9 8 7 6 5 4 3 2 1

Other books by Eric Wilson

The Tom and Liz Austen Mysteries

Also available by Eric Wilson

This book is dedicated to my uncles,
Bruce Wilson and Cayley Wilson,
who lost their lives in the Second World War

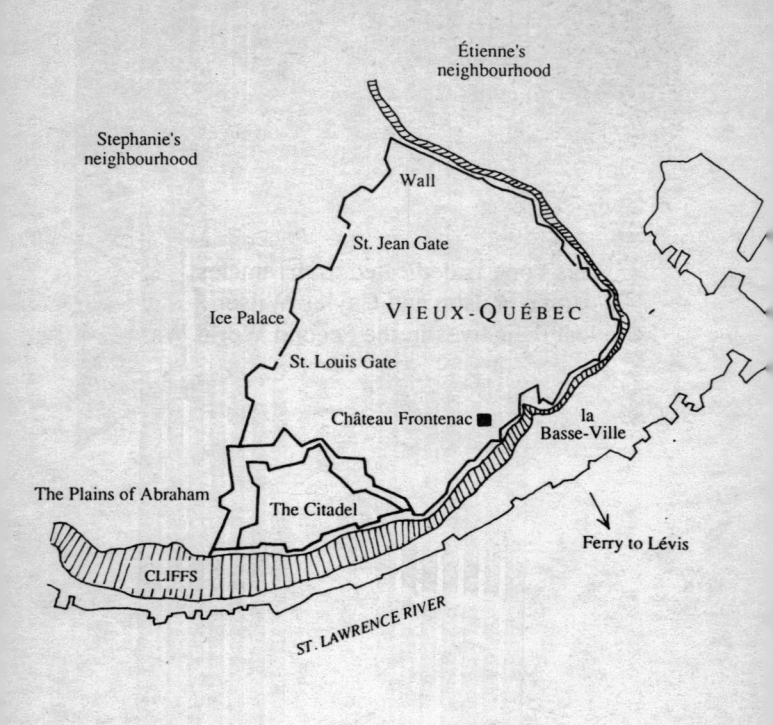

1

Tom Austen leaned into a cold wind.

He was in Baie St-Paul, a small town in rural Quebec. It was night-time, and snow gusted down a street that seemed hundreds of years old. Wooden houses with big porches stood along the winding road, their yards full of trees with bare branches.

But one thing didn't fit. A small, white car had just passed Tom, its wheels crunching along the icy street. The car windows were smokey-black, hiding its occupants inside, and there was an aerial for a cellular phone.

The car slowed as it passed Tom. He could sense eyes staring at him, then the car moved away. At the same time, Tom saw a woman in a red ski jacket and jeans coming out of the night, walking toward a telephone booth. Again, the car slowed down while passing her, then crossed a small bridge and stopped at a gas station that was closed for the night. The headlights went off and the car became something that was watching.

The woman didn't seem to notice. She dropped her cigarette in the snow, took out a slip of paper, then punched at the phone buttons. As Tom passed the booth, heading into the confectionary beside it, he could hear her speaking.

"Listen. . . ." Her voice was determined. "I gave you 12 hours to agree to an interview. You haven't come through. No interview, so now I break the story. Your name is about to be mud."

Tom glanced at the woman as he entered the store. She was about 45, with a narrow face and small eyes behind thick horn-rimmed glasses. A lighter flared in her hand as she lit another cigarette, then she squinted against the smoke, listening intently to the person she'd called.

The air inside the store was warm. A man with a grey moustache and a friendly smile was behind the counter, watching television. The store was exactly like the one near Tom's home in Winnipeg, but most things were in French. His first evening in Baie St-Paul he'd wandered up and down the aisles, homesick, staring at the English side of the labels on toothpaste packages. Then he'd enjoyed a few games on the store's video machine and felt better.

The man smiled at him. "*Hé bien, Pee Wee. C'était vraiment un bon match, hier soir!*"

Tom mumbled a reply, unable to follow the man's quick French. He was crazy about hockey, and had been in the stands for both exhibition games between Winnipeg and the local Pee Wee team, whose coach was a friend of Tom's coach. Winnipeg was playing exhibition games here before competing in Quebec City's famous Pee Wee tournament. Teams from all over North America and as far away as Japan and the Soviet Union would be playing.

Headlights glared against the store windows. Tom looked up the street and saw the white car moving away from the gas station. It crossed the bridge over a small, frozen stream. The street was empty.

The woman in the phone booth was still talking, her breath clouding in the cold air. She didn't seem to notice the approaching car.

This time the driver's window was down. He looked about 25, with sallow skin and black hair pulled back into a small ponytail. Under his left eye was the tattoo of a dagger. The skin around the tattoo was red and looked sore.

In the passenger seat was a woman, but she was difficult to see in the car's dark interior. Tom had an impression of blonde hair and unusually large eyes. Then he saw the driver lifting a fisted hand to his mouth. Tom thought the man was about to cough, but he saw that the fist was curled around a small tube. It was aimed at the woman talking in the phone booth.

Tom saw her wince. As the car sped away down the street she lifted a hand to her neck. "Sir," Tom said to the man. "*Monsieur* . . . uh . . . help! Something's wrong out there! Please, call the police."

"*La police*?"

"*Oui!* Yes—and hurry!"

Tom rushed outside. The cold wind cut through him, and even the toque and gloves he wore didn't help warm him. In the phone booth the woman was staring at a small silver dart.

"Strange," she said, as Tom approached. "This thing hit me in the neck." She flicked the dart away into the snow. "Some kid must have been fooling around with an air rifle."

"No," Tom exclaimed. "It was a man. He was watching you from his car, then he shot you with that dart."

The woman looked up and down the street, then at Tom. "Are you certain that's what happened?"

"Yes!"

"What did that guy look like?"

"Well, kind of a dark complexion. He had a ponytail, and a dagger tattooed under his eye. There was a woman with him. The car's licence plate was hidden behind some snow, but I saw an aerial for a cellular phone. I thought maybe they were talking to you."

"No, I was speaking to. . . ." She touched her forehead. "All of a sudden I've got an awful headache." She looked at the phone. "My call. I. . . ." Reaching for the receiver, she swayed to one side and had to steady herself with a hand. Shaking her head, she looked at Tom. Her eyes seemed cloudy.

"Where. . . ?" Again she shook her head. "Once I was in a city, somewhere. . . . I remember the sky, how. . . ." She put a hand to her forehead, and then her knees gave out and she fell.

Tom gasped in shock. She was dead.

2

The man came out of his store.

"*Mais, qu'est-ce qu'elle à? Elle est . . . malade?*"

Tom's fingers were pressed to the woman's neck, searching in vain for a pulse. Standing up, he grabbed the phone receiver. "Who's there?"

Someone at the other end was listening, but didn't speak. Then, with a click, the line went dead.

Tom looked at the man. "Did you call the police?"

"*Oui.*" He raised his head. "*Écoute.*" Carried on the

Blue and red flashes lit the night, growing stronger as the police raced to the scene. Car doors slammed and officers ran toward Tom and the man, who stood over the body. As an ambulance arrived, and police lines were set up to keep curious onlookers away, a woman wearing the stripes of a senior officer began questioning Tom and the store owner. "I'd met this woman," the officer said. "She arrived in town last week, to stay with her niece for awhile. This is a small town so most people know each other."

The store owner said, "*Marie-Claire est venue chez moi pour me poser des questions sur l'Enclave.*"

Tom looked at the officer. "What's he saying?"

"That the dead woman had been asking about the Enclave."

"What's that?"

"A new manufacturing plant outside of town. They make chemical fertilizers."

"Why'd she ask questions about it?"

"Marie-Claire Jasmin was an investigative journalist. That means a reporter who sniffs out secrets. If the story is hot, a scandal results and the reporter becomes famous. Marie-Claire was well known for the secrets she'd uncovered in cities like Montreal and Toronto. Some people here thought she was investigating the Enclave."

"A plant producing fertilizers has a secret? That doesn't seem likely."

The officer watched a stretcher crew lift their burden into the ambulance, then turned to a uniformed man beside her. "*Et sa nièce? Quelqu'un devrait lui apprendre la nouvelle.*"

He looked at his notes. "*Elle s'appelle Michelle Jasmin.*"

"Hey," Tom exclaimed. "I know Michelle! She was at the hockey game last night. My age, beautiful long hair, right?"

The man nodded. "The dead woman was Michelle's aunt."

Tom looked down the street, remembering the night before. He and his billet had walked home with a few local kids, including Michelle. She'd mentioned an aunt staying at the house until her parents returned from a trip to Europe.

Now Michelle was in the house alone, and that white car could still be around.

"Are you going to give Michelle police protection?"

"Certainly," the woman replied. "As soon as we get finished here, I'll go over to her house."

Again Tom looked down the street, picturing Michelle alone. After asking the officers if they were finished with him, he started walking. People still stood on their porches, arms crossed, calling information to their neighbours. Tom hurried down the street under a sky that was bright with stars, listening to bells sounding from the spire of a floodlit church.

Michelle was surprised to see him. "Tom, how pleasant! It was so good to meet you last night." Her eyes were dark brown, bright and intelligent, and her chestnut-coloured hair fell in thick, soft waves down her back. Tom followed her into a comfortable living room where people on a TV screen were talking in French.

"Michelle, I . . . there's something . . . about your aunt, she. . . ."

Telling Michelle was the toughest thing Tom had ever done. She was still crying when someone knocked on the front door.

Tom parted the curtains. "It's that police officer. I can see her car."

As Michelle answered questions, speaking in rapid French, tears ran from her eyes. Then she turned to Tom. "I must leave for Quebec City. *Ma soeur*, my sister, lives there. This officer has said I am probably not at risk but she would like me in the city with my sister. A night bus will depart before long."

"When are your parents coming home?"

"Soon — perhaps only a few days."

"I'll be in Quebec City, too. How can I find you?" Tom wrote down the phone number, then looked at the officer. "Okay if I stay with Michelle until she gets the bus?"

"That is a good idea. A taxi will soon be here. I want Michelle to take it to the bus stop."

Within 15 minutes they were in the taxi, travelling along icy streets past darkened houses. Michelle was still crying softly, but she wiped away her tears while listening to Tom and the taxi driver talk about the Enclave. "People here do not feel good about that place," Michelle said. "There are no jobs available in the Enclave. All workers come from other places and live behind fences of barbed wire. Only one local person is working there."

"Who's that?" Tom asked Michelle.

"A man with the name Gaston. He is a chef, cooking meals for the workers inside the Enclave."

"Hey, I've met him. He's a neighbour of my billet. His clothes smell of cigarette smoke."

She nodded. "Oui, that is Gaston. An excellent chef but an unhappy man. He lives alone. So *triste*."

"My billet says Gaston's been acting strangely lately. Really paranoid, afraid someone's going to get him."

"But why?"

"I don't know," Tom replied. "Maybe he told your aunt a secret about the Enclave. She was probably working on a big story that would have made her even more famous."

"Fame was not my aunt's goal in life. She just tried to make the world a better place." Michelle brushed away more tears. "I loved her so much."

Tom squeezed her hand, then looked out at the houses lining the street. "Your aunt gave someone 12 hours to agree to an interview. Maybe that person ordered her death. The guy in the white car shot the dart, but I bet he was working for someone with a secret to protect."

As the taxi driver unloaded Michelle's bags, Tom stamped his feet against the cold. Minutes later, big headlights cut the night as a bus arrived, its sign reading QUÉBEC EXPRESS. "Sit near the driver," he suggested. "And switch off the reading light over your head. That'll be safer."

Michelle smiled and touched his hand. "You care about me, Tom. *Merci — j'apprécie beaucoup*."

"Listen, I'll phone you when I get to Quebec City. My team's got only one exhibition game left here."

"I would like that, Tom. *Bonne chance* with the hockey game tomorrow against my Baie St-Paul friends. Now I will be cheering for both teams."

Tom watched as Michelle climbed into the bus and found a seat by herself. She leaned close to the glass, waving. Under the reading light her headband was a soft pink. Then she flicked off the light, and the bus pulled away into the darkness.

* * *

Arriving back at his billet, Tom studied the neighbouring house where the chef lived. It was small and white, and stood alone in the middle of an enormous yard drifted with thick snow. A plume of smoke rose from the chimney but the windows were dark.

Tom's billet opened the door of his house. "*Salut*, Tom," he called. "Are you coming inside? People have been phoning, saying you were at the store with the police. We are anxious to hear what happened."

"I'll be in right away, Hubert."

Tom took a final look at the chef's lonely house, then went inside. Hubert's parents waited in the living room, looking anxious. *Monsieur* Ferron was a gentle man whose nose was usually deep in a book, and *Madame* Ferron was an artist. As Tom ate homemade bread covered with maple syrup, and drank hot chocolate, they asked him a lot of questions.

"What a terrible event," Mme Ferron said. "Something is wrong about the Enclave. I have not liked that place since it was built."

M. Ferron smiled. "We have discussed this before, *ma chérie*. Your imagination is running away."

"*Vraiment?* Then why the imported workers? Why the barbed wire fence around the Enclave? Why the trucks arriving and leaving only at night? What do the trucks carry that is so secret?"

"*Ma chérie, ma chérie.* You are much too excitable." M. Ferron clapped his hands. "*Allez*, Hubert and Tom. Straight into bed. Tomorrow is the final game for the Winnipeg Pee Wees and Baie St-Paul. Our two favourite players must get their rest, and so must their fans."

Tom followed Hubert upstairs. Alone in his room, he stood at the window studying the chef's wooden house, surrounded by deep drifts and dark, bare trees. Even though it had two floors, the house looked small in the middle of all that snow. Then Tom crawled under the bed's cozy duvet and stared at the patterns of moonlight on his ceiling, thinking about Michelle and her aunt and

Gaston, then about the white car and its driver with the tattoo.

Finally Tom fell into a deep sleep where he dreamed about a little wooden house alone in the trees. Standing at a fireplace, he warmed his hands over the flames. Tom shifted in his sleep. The crackling of the flames was so loud that he opened his eyes.

The moonlight patterns were gone from the ceiling, replaced by flickering red and orange light. Tom rolled over, glancing at the window, then sat straight up, horrified.

The chef's house was on fire.

3

Tom pulled on his clothes and raced downstairs to the porch. *Madame* Ferron was already on the phone to the fire department, and Hubert was putting on snowshoes.

"The chef is in trouble, Tom!"

Quickly he also strapped on snowshoes. The burning house made the snow appear red. The boys raced across the drifts, then saw an upstairs window explode out, followed by billowing smoke.

"Is that Gaston's bedroom?"

"No — he sleeps downstairs."

Water was dripping off icicles melting in the heat. Tom slammed into the buckled front door with his shoulder, smashing it open. Hubert rubbed snow on a toque and a scarf, handed one to Tom, and they ran into the building with this protection over their mouths and noses. The flames hadn't yet reached the lower part of the house, but smoke stung Tom's eyes as he followed Hubert down a dark hallway.

The chef lay on his bed in pajamas, breathing with a strange sound. He didn't respond to Tom's first-aid attempts so finally the boys carried him from the burning house, thankful he was a small man, and wrapped him in a blanket when they were safely outside.

''Hey!'' Tom stared into the nearby trees. The fire's fierce light showed a face watching them from behind a tree. Once again Tom strapped on his snowshoes, then hurried toward the woods. In the shelter of the trees, where the snow wasn't as deep, recent footprints showed the trail of the person Tom had spotted.

Somewhere in the night an owl cried, making Tom's skin prickle. The snowshoes were clumsy on his feet as he moved forward, trying to follow the man's trail, then he heard the thump of a car door closing.

Hurrying to the top of a nearby ridge, Tom saw a car driving away into the snowy darkness. He was positive it was the same white car he'd seen earlier.

*   *   *

Tom woke early the next morning. Quietly leaving the house, he walked along the snow-packed road past the black ruins of the chef's home. Down by the river, on the outskirts of the small town, a fishing boat was moored for the winter, surrounded by ice. Across the road from it was the large house where Tom's coach and some of the other boys were billeted. When he arrived there he found them sitting around a long wooden table in the kitchen, shovelling down a huge breakfast.

Tom's coach hadn't yet poured his first cup of coffee so he was still grumpy, but after hearing about the events of the previous night he accepted Tom's request to miss the final exhibition game against Baie St-Paul, so he could take the bus to Quebec City and check on Michelle's safety.

Dietmar Oban looked up from buttering a stack of toast. "Hey, Austen, tell us about Michelle. Is she one of the girls who were hanging around the arena last night after the game?"

Jesse Silsbe smiled. "She's the one who asked for your autograph, right?"

"Michelle didn't mean it," Tom protested, as everyone laughed. "She was just kidding."

"Then you and your billet took off with those cute girls. The rest of us got the thrill of walking home with Coach."

The man patted the round tummy that stretched the fabric of his sweater. "My wife still thinks I'm cute. It's my personal opinion she's absolutely right."

"Well, Austen?" Dietmar demanded. "Did you give her an autograph?"

Tom grinned. "That's privileged information. You'll have to ask Michelle."

Pale light was finally creeping into the morning sky as Tom left the house and returned toward town, huddled in his jacket for warmth. A slow-moving car approached, its driver studying Tom. "Hey," she said, leaning out the window. She was in her forties, with a round face and round eyes, and hair turning grey. "You're Tom Austen, right? I was just at your billet, looking for you. They told me to try down here." She nodded at the passenger door. "Hop in."

"No thanks."

Tom kept walking as the car crept along at his side. "My name's Alexis Alexander," the driver said. "I'm a reporter from Toronto. I've been working in Quebec City with Marie-Claire on her new investigation. She phoned me two days ago, really excited because the chef was going to give her inside information about the Enclave. It sounded like he knew something really important.''

''Any idea what it was?''

She shook her head. ''Marie-Claire didn't phone again, then last night I heard she'd been murdered. And now the chef.''

''He isn't dead, he's in a coma.''

''What did Michelle tell you about her aunt? Does she have any idea why Marie-Claire died?''

Tom studied the woman's eyes. The car was still crunching slowly along at his side. A tiny tape recorder lay on the front seat, its cassette turning. ''Are you recording me?'' he asked.

She glanced at the machine. ''You've got sharp eyes, Tom.''

He didn't say anything more as Alexis Alexander continued to ask questions, keeping the car at his side all the way to the Ferrons' house. Tom thought about her while packing his gear in the house, and didn't relax until he boarded the bus for Quebec City.

The only available seat was right at the front, next to a man who said his name was Reg and his job was writing television programmes. As Reg told stories about his life the bus rolled through the countryside, then curved down a hill above the river. Out the window Tom could see an icebreaker cutting a channel along the frozen St. Lawrence. Close by the river were the tall spires of a huge cathedral.

''Ste Anne de Beaupré,'' said the driver. ''The famous shrine. Hanging inside are the crutches and braces of those cured by miracles.''

"Okay to stop and see?" Tom asked the driver as they drove past the cathedral.

The man shook his head. "*Désolé, mais* this isn't the Gray Line." He whistled through his teeth as the bus zoomed along the highway, which was now bordered by motels, gas stations and restaurants. "There is the Île d'Orléans." He gestured at an island in the wide St. Lawrence. "That is where the General Wolfe of the English assembled his forces, before attacking the French defenders of Quebec City."

"We studied that in school."

"The British rained cannonballs down on the city, weakening the defences. But, high on the cliff, it remained difficult to attack. Then late one night the English boats drifted silently along the cliffs to a landing place usually used by the French to unload supplies."

"I heard that a soldier yelled in French, *Long Live the King!* fooling the sentries into letting let them past. What a classic move!"

"By morning the English army had climbed to the Plains of Abraham and defeated the city's defenders. So the English took control, and to this day, on Canada's money and stamps, is the British monarch."

"How do you feel about that? I mean, you know, since you're French."

The driver smiled. "I could write a book about how I feel."

The bus was approaching Quebec City. Many of its streets were beside the river, and others were on the heights above. The city's high cliffs were dominated by an enormous building that looked like a castle in Europe. "Is that the fort they defended?"

"No. You are looking at the Château Frontenac, a hotel."

Reg shook his head. "I'm disappointed. I thought that was the castle of some old baron. You know, full of dusty furniture and ghost stories."

"I guess you have heard about the meetings this week in Quebec City between the American president and the head of the Soviet Union? Those two bigshots will both be staying in the Château Frontenac while they sign the agreement to ban the manufacture of chemical weapons."

"Wow," Reg said. "Imagine the security! Plus the winter carnival opens tonight, with thousands of visitors jamming the streets. Why'd they hold the summit meeting at the same time as the carnival?"

The driver shook his head. "I do not know. The two leaders insisted on signing the agreement in Canada. Kind of a salute to the Canadian efforts for peace."

"But why meet in a hotel? Because it's built like a fortress?"

"I guess so. During the last world war there was also a summit meeting in the Château Frontenac. Maybe government leaders are inspired by the view."

"Why aren't they meeting in the States or the USSR?"

"I believe such leaders often meet in more neutral countries like Iceland or Canada."

"Well, I think it's great those guys are coming here in search of peace." Turning, Reg grinned at Tom. "Your first visit to Quebec City?"

"Yes sir. My team's playing in the Pee Wee hockey tournament."

"Hey! Maybe I'm sitting beside the NHL's next megastar."

Tom laughed. "I doubt it."

The bus angled down an off-ramp and entered a street of stores and office buildings. High above them on the cliff towered the Château Frontenac with its hundreds of windows and green roof.

"That is a copper roof," the driver explained. "The aging process turned it green." He pointed at a wall that ran along the top of the cliff. "That wall was built centuries ago and surrounds the ancient heart of the city, which is called *Vieux Québec.*"

"How'd you pronounce that?" Reg asked.

"*Vieux* means old. Pronounce it *view*, as in *look at the nice view.*"

Inside the bus depot Tom met his new billet, Étienne Ducharme, and his father. They both wore Québec Nordiques pins, buttons and toques. Grinning, Étienne shook hands.

"Thursday, first game my Pee Wee team. Against you, Tom, against Winnipeg. What exciting start to tournament!"

Tom flipped through his pocket English-French dictionary, seeking words. "Um . . . *emplacement?* . . . uh, what . . . ?"

"I am goalie. And you?"

As Tom laboured over an answer in French they got into the family's car and drove along narrow streets, where the houses stood shoulder-to-shoulder with their front doors opening directly on to the sidewalk. Some houses looked like old Christmas cards with smoke lazily rising from their stone chimneys, while others had been more recently built. Snow drifted down on the people trudging home at the end of a long day.

Étienne and his parents lived in a house that was 152 years old. Tom carried his suitcase up curving wooden stairs, grooved by many generations of feet, to a room with a low ceiling and a small window thick with frost.

"Our ancestors were not big people," M. Ducharme laughed. "Now, come for delicious food."

Étienne's mother had a beaming face and spoke no English. Throughout the meal she gestured for Tom to eat more and more. They had chicken, rice, salad, and chocolate cake with ice cream. Later, after Tom and Étienne had done the dishes, they went into the living room, where the Ducharmes were waiting to show a video that featured Étienne's career on skates from his shakiest early days.

While Tom watched the video his lap was suddenly filled by the family cat, *Poil-de-Carotte*, meaning Carrot-Fur. He was big and friendly, and very proud of his bushy orange tail. Afterwards, Tom again tried to reach Michelle on the phone, and this time succeeded. They arranged to meet at the Ice Palace later that evening.

''We shall drop you there,'' M. Ducharme offered. ''We go for the night to relatives across the river in Lévis. You will be safe here alone, Tom, or will you come to Lévis?''

''No thanks—I'll be fine.''

As Tom put on his jacket he looked up the curving staircase, thinking about being alone in the house. Then he shivered, wondering if he'd just made a mistake.

4

The Ice Palace was amazing. Built each year just for the Carnival, it resembled a huge sugar-cube castle. Pink spotlights glowed on the walls and flags fluttered high above the battlements.

A large crowd had gathered to party. The people danced together to the music from big speakers, laughed and talked, and examined nearby ice sculptures while waiting for the carnival's opening ceremonies to begin.

Tom's favourite ice sculpture showed a creature from outer space, with mysterious eyes and a head tapering to a white point. Beyond the party was the floodlit, green roof of the Château Frontenac. Tom imagined the hotel's security preparations, with the two presidents about to meet within those fortress-like walls.

"Tom!"

Michelle came out of the night. She was wearing her pink ski jacket and a pair of jeans. "It is good to see you again."

"How are you feeling, Michelle?"

"I have cried a lot." She shook her head. "It is so *difficile*. I have talked to my sister for hours and that has helped. So has your friendship, Tom."

"That's good to know."

They turned to look at the Ice Palace as *Salut Bonhomme* sounded from the speakers and a huge snowman appeared on stage. This was Bonhomme, the symbol of the carnival. Wearing his trademark red toque, big grin and long sash, Bonhomme danced along the stage, clapping his hands to the music. The crowd cheered, and the excitement increased.

Soon after, seven young women in flowing white cloaks were escorted on stage by Bonhomme. One of these duchesses would be crowned *la Reine du Carnaval* tonight. As they spoke into a microphone Michelle translated for Tom.

"How'd you get so good in English?" he asked.

She smiled. "I try hard in school. My goal is to work someday at the United Nations."

As the Queen was crowned and fireworks exploded across the sky, Michelle took Tom's arm. "I want to show you this beautiful city." She led him through an arched gate in the city wall and they entered ancient, narrow streets where warm light glowed from the windows of houses with stone walls.

"Welcome to *Vieux Québec*, Tom."

He smiled. "What a wonderful way to see it for the first time."

For a while they wandered the streets in friendly silence. Then Tom looked at Michelle. "I'm really sorry about your aunt."

"*Merci*. It is so sad."

"Listen, did she ever mention a reporter called Alexis Alexander?"

"*Certainement*. I have met Alexis at my home in Baie St-Paul."

"I don't trust her. She was taping me." Tom described what had happened, including the fire at the chef's. "The police think someone got into Gaston's house, drugged him and then set the fire. But they can't learn anything until he's out of the coma." A group of chattering people squeezed past, each person holding *Carnaval* balloons. "I wonder what Gaston told your aunt."

"I'll check her notebook. Maybe. . . ."

"You've got it?"

"Yes, it seemed safest to keep the notebook until we learn more. I put it in my suitcase before leaving for Quebec City."

"When can you read it?"

"Tonight."

"Then let's meet again tomorrow." As Michelle smiled at him with her brown eyes, Tom felt himself blushing. He grinned. "Well, it's a good enough excuse."

Michelle laughed, and they continued along the street until they reached the security zone around the Château Frontenac. Here the streets crawled with police while soldiers patrolled the rooftops.

Michelle looked in the window of a small shop at a mannequin dressed in a princess gown. "Tom, that is the exact costume I wear to Mardi Gras."

"What's that?"

"Mardi Gras is terribly special event for *Carnaval*. A dinner and dance at a lovely hotel, with many people in costume. My sister has invited me. Please come as my escort, Tom."

"Thanks, I'd really like that. Do I get to wear a costume, too?"

She nodded. "Tomorrow we can arrange something with this shop."

"Great."

Winding streets led Michelle and Tom to the cliff edge, where they looked at the streets and houses far below. A ferry was just beginning its journey across the river to Lévis on the far shore. "I'd like to take that trip," Tom said. "I love any kind of travelling. Except skateboards since a friend of mine snapped his ankle."

Michelle asked Tom about the accident, then looked at her watch. "I am late! *Merci*, Tom. It was a good time. Meet you at the costume shop tomorrow at 2 p.m., okay?"

"Perfect." Tom watched her hurry away under the streetlights. Tomorrow at 2 p.m. seemed a long time to wait.

*   *   *

Tom kept thinking about Michelle as he returned to *la Basse-Ville*, the lower town, and followed a long street of stores with bright *Carnaval* decorations adorning their windows. After passing a building with a familiar red roof and a sign reading *Poulet frit à la Kentucky*, he paused to watch the swift moves of a bunch of boys playing hockey on a floodlit outdoor rink, then walked on to Étienne's house.

All the windows were dark. The house looked lonely, with the family away in Lévis for the night. The air inside was chilly. Tom made sure the door was bolted, then said goodnight to Carrot-Fur, who was curled up on a chair in the living room.

Tom sighed, wishing now he wasn't spending the night alone in a 152-year-old house with a spiral staircase that creaked. He'd found a copy of the local newspaper, and now crumpled the pages as he went up to his room. He'd been thinking about Gaston the chef, out cold on his bed with the fire creeping closer, and knew he needed a good defence if he wanted to sleep.

Outside Tom's window, snow drifted down on the roof-tops of nearby houses. He was lonely. He looked at his plane ticket, thinking about home, then sat on the bed and wrote in his notebook. He didn't have much information about the driver of the white car, except the sore-looking skin around the tattoo of the dagger. Did that mean the man had been recently tattooed?

Tom wrote *tattoo parlour in QC?* in his notebook, then sighed again and made sure his bed was completely protected by crumpled newspapers. If anyone approached while he slept, the crackling of newspapers underfoot would instantly awaken him.

Tom blew out the candle beside his bed. The smell of hot wax filled the darkness as he slipped into a dream of racing on snowshoes across red drifts. After awhile he awoke with a start, then fell asleep again. In his dream he was pounding his shoulder against the door of the chef's house, over and over, when suddenly he sat up in the darkness and cried out. *The newspapers were crackling.*

*   *   *

Tom leapt out of bed, yelling.

It was totally dark in the room. He stumbled into the hallway and crashed down the spiral staircase to the tele-phone on the floor below. Switching on a lamp, he waited breathlessly to be connected to Emergency. No more noises came from above. The house was absolutely silent.

"Police? Hello, *police?* Listen, I need help!"

Tom babbled his address, then added, "It could be arson — call the fire department!" Hanging up, he saw something move on the spiral staircase above. Two huge eyes looked at him over the edge of the stairs. Loud purring sounded.

"Carrot-Fur? Was that *you* upstairs? Making the newspapers crackle?" Tom stared at the phone, then grabbed it in a desperate attempt to stop the emergency squad. But, even as a voice answered, he heard the wail of approaching sirens.

"Oh no," Tom whispered. Brakes squealed outside and car doors slammed. "Oh no! I don't believe this."

*   *   *

Snow gusted off a rooftop and down Tom's neck as he was escorted to a police car. After an unhappy drive he was led by unsmiling officers into the police station and taken down a series of corridors to a big room, where officers worked over phones and computers.

While Tom was being questioned, an office door opened and four people came out: a woman and three men. Approaching the officers, they asked some questions in French. Then the woman turned to Tom and said in English, "I understand your cat, *Poil-de-Carotte*, has caused some trouble. The officers are a bit on edge because of the big crowds here for *Carnaval*. They thought you might be a carnival wiseguy, playing a trick on them. Will you accept their apologies?"

"Apologies! Sure—I owe them! I was just worried they were going to send me to prison."

Smiling, the woman held out a hand. She was about 50, with blue eyes and beautifully styled hair. Her business suit looked expensive, and she wore some nice jewellery. "My name's Commissioner Martin. I'm originally from the west myself. My husband is a government Senator, and I'm a police commissioner." She introduced the men. "We commissioners represent the people of the city at police headquarters, making sure everything runs smoothly. We've just completed a meeting about security for the summit at the Château Frontenac."

Tom told them about being involved in the events at Baie St-Paul. Commissioner Martin said she hadn't yet read the reports on the case, and asked Tom for details. As he began describing his chase after the mystery person in the woods outside the chef's burning house, a phone rang. Tom stopped speaking as Commissioner Martin spoke briefly, then hung up.

"The media's demanding interviews about the dead woman. Apparently she was from Quebec City." She looked at Tom. "What happened after you spotted the white car?"

"Nothing much. It drove away through the woods, but I'm sure it was the same car. It even had the cellular phone aerial."

One of the other commissioners looked at Tom. He wore a three-piece suit and had a handsome face with curly brown hair. "Are you related to Ted Austen, an Inspector with the Winnipeg police?"

"Yes, sir. He's my Dad."

"I guess you're here for the hockey tournament and *Carnaval*. I will phone Ted, tell him what has happened."

Commissioner Martin took out a business card with her name printed on it. "I'll write my personal phone number on this card. It's 367-3787. If you need help, please don't hesitate to call." She studied Tom. "We're always looking for talent in this police force. Contact me when you're older if you decide to get into your Dad's line of work."

"Thanks!" Tom stared at Commissioner Martin's name in golden letters on the card. "What an honour."

"You impress me." She looked at the others. "We'll meet again tomorrow morning. I'm still worried about some of the security details for the summit. Having the American and Soviet presidents together in this city could be a nightmare."

5

The next day Tom was feeling great as Michelle approached in a parka, long hair blowing in the cold wind.

"Hi Tom. *Ça fait du bien de le voir.* How are you?"

"Great." He felt suddenly shy. "How are you feeling today? I mean, about your aunt?"

"Thank you for asking. It will take time for the pain to go." She smiled. "But seeing you again makes me happy."

After arranging for Tom's Mardi Gras costume they walked to McDonald's. There was a babble of voices inside as people talked to each other and counter assistants called out orders; one cried something in French that Tom, smiling, was sure meant *Can I help somebody down here, please?* Then he looked at the menu. *"I'm having Poulet McCroquettes.* What a great name.''

They carried their trays upstairs and sat beside big windows that overlooked the crowded streets of *Vieux Québec.* Munching their food, Tom and Michelle watched the excited people. Some blew blasts on long plastic horns, while others danced together, or looked in shop windows. Then a van stopped, and everyone applauded when Bonhomme appeared from inside.

"I love that big snowman," Tom said. "He's kind of the symbol of *Carnaval,* right?''

Michelle nodded. "He is driven all over the city, making appearances. Kids get so excited to meet Bonhomme in person! See how he is grinning, and always dancing? Such energy is needed from the actor inside the costume.''

Tom told her about the Carrot-Fur incident, and was pleased that the story made her laugh. "So, what about your aunt's notes? Learn anything?''

"Yes. Something about Seron. Her scrawl is *difficile* to read, but that is the name. My sister runs a computer search on the word Seron this very day.''

"Anything else?''

Michelle nodded. "I believe someone called Z is involved. The initial appears in my aunt's notes several times.''

"Maybe Z's the driver of the white car.''

Leaving McDonald's they looked up as a chopper roared across their heads. Inside were vigilant faces, scanning the crowds. "Security for the summit," Tom shouted above the noise. "The American and Soviet presidents are meeting in the Château Frontenac this week. They're going to sign a protocol to ban the manufacturing of chemical weapons. With luck, no more will ever be made.''

"I hope the leaders will be safe in Quebec City. Peace is so important.''

"Michelle, is there a tattoo parlour here?"

She shook her head. "I have no idea. Why?"

"The driver of the white car had a tattoo on his face. The skin around it was red, so I thought maybe the tattoo was new. If so, it could have been done in Quebec City."

"You have a good mind, Tom."

He smiled at her. "Listen, maybe you could come to the *Carnaval* parade. I was lucky—my name came up in a special draw so I'll be on the Pee Wee hockey float."

"*Félicitations*. It will be wonderful to see you."

"There'll be guys from several countries on the float. My billet, Étienne Ducharme, also got selected. This morning we each had a face-scan done on a computer. I actually saw my skull outlined on the screen."

"What is the face-scan for?"

"There's a special security zone on the parade route. When each float enters the zone, infra-red cameras will scan the faces. The computer will analyze each face and alert security if it doesn't match."

"Why the security?"

"Nobody's sure, but it's probably because of the summit."

As they were looking at an ice sculpture of life-size mountain goats, Tom and Michelle were abruptly pushed aside by a passing woman. Then she turned to stare at Michelle.

"Hey, Michelle! *Tu ne te souviens pas de moi?* I'm Alexis Alexander. I worked with your aunt. Listen, I'm sure Marie-Claire kept a notebook on this investigation. Have you got it?"

"Why?"

"Because I want to see it. I'm determined to find the person who killed your aunt. It'll make a great story."

"You would not try to find the killer for the sake of my aunt?"

"Sure, sweetie. That, too." Alexis Alexander unwrapped a stick of spearmint gum and popped it into her mouth. "So, where's the notebook? I'm in kind of a hurry."

Michelle shook her head. "I am sorry you do not care about my poor aunt." She took Tom's arm. "*Allons-nous-en!*"

Tom sensed the anger radiating from Alexis Alexander as they walked rapidly away. "Did she really work with your aunt?"

Michelle nodded. "She has a brilliant mind. My aunt called Alexis the number one reporter in Canada."

"Then put that notebook somewhere safe."

She smiled. "I have already."

Tom kicked at the snow with his boot. "Listen, any chance you'd come to my first hockey game? It's tomorrow."

"*J'aimerais ça.*" At the corner of Rue St-Jean, the street where Michelle was living, she said good bye to Tom. "I will look forward to your game."

"Great, Michelle. See you there."

Tom watched her walk away along the snowy street, feeling happy they'd met.

*   *   *

Reaching his billet in *la Basse-Ville*, at the foot of the cliff, Tom was let into the house by *Madame* Ducharme. To his surprise, his luggage and hockey equipment had been piled in the hallway.

"Hey! What's going on?"

Mme Ducharme shook her head. "*Désolée, Tom, mais je ne parle pas anglais.*"

"My stuff! Why's it here in the hall? I'm not leaving for at least five days!"

"*Je ne te comprends pas.*"

"My stuff! What's going on?"

Someone was knocking on the front door. A man stood there in a black chauffeur's uniform. "Mr. Austen?"

"Uh, yes. Yes, I'm Tom Austen."

"Would you come with me?" He stepped to the curb and opened the door of a limousine. Tom saw leather seats and a TV set. The chauffeur clicked on a VCR, and a woman's face appeared on the screen.

"Hi Tom." She was smiling. "I'm Commissioner Martin. We met last night at the police station. After what happened at your billet — and knowing you're concerned about the arsonist — I decided that it would be better if you stay with my family."

Tom looked back at *Madame* Ducharme, standing in the doorway with a friendly smile on her face. Her meal last night had left his taste buds aching for more.

"So," Commissioner Martin said from the TV screen, "hop into the limousine. I'm looking forward to introducing my daughter. She's your age, and smart like you. People say she's really quite pretty."

Tom smiled at Mme Ducharme. "I've got a new billet. But it's been great, thanks. I'll see Étienne when our teams play tomorrow." When he realized she didn't understand what he was saying, he gestured that he was going in the limousine and that he'd be okay. Mme Ducharme said something in French and waved as Tom got into the limo. As it slipped away from the curb, he tried the TV set's channel zapper, then got some apple juice from the small refrigerator and put on a CD. Leaning back in the soft leather seat, listening to the music booming from hidden speakers, Tom felt totally relaxed as the city streets slid silently past outside.

Too soon, the ride was over. The limo pulled into a driveway that curved up to a large brick house with pillars beside the front door. As the driver leapt out to open Tom's door, a girl his own age appeared on the porch. Her short black hair was swept back from her face and her eyes were large; she wore a ski jacket over a Polo sweatshirt and designer jeans.

"Hi, Tom!" she said. "I'm Stephanie Martin. Mom's told me lots about you. What sign are you?"

"Libra."

"I'm Scorpio. Listen, what was it like dragging that chef out of his burning house?"

"I wouldn't want to repeat the experience. I've been feeling kind of tense about fire ever since."

Hearing sirens, Tom turned to see police motorcycles approaching with flashing lights. Then a remarkably long limousine stopped in the driveway and the chauffeur rushed to open the passenger door for a distinguished man with grey hair. "That's my Dad," Stephanie said. "He's a Senator in the government."

The Senator was followed by his wife, Commissioner Martin. There were diamonds on her ears and fingers and she wore a beautiful green coat. She smiled at Tom and said hello, then introduced her husband and a second man who'd also stepped from the limousine.

"This is our guest, Mr. Smith."

He wore a three-piece grey suit and had an unusual handshake. Taking off his sunglasses, Mr. Smith studied Tom with steely eyes.

"So this is Tom Austen. How interesting to meet you."

6

"We were just at the Château Frontenac," Commissioner Martin said.

"What was it like?" Stephanie demanded. "Was the American president nice? What about the Soviet leader?" She turned to Tom. "My parents just welcomed the leaders to Quebec City."

Commissioner Martin smiled. "The mayor welcomed them officially, dear. We were just guests."

"We should get out of the cold," said the Senator. He was older than his wife. His face was lean and his eyes very blue, but they looked sad to Tom.

Inside, one wall of the large living room was entirely mirrored. It reflected the burning flames of a fireplace and also the furniture, which was made of beautiful woods and fabrics. Bushes and small trees grew in gigantic porcelain tubs, and most of the hardwood floor was covered by an immense carpet with a striking pattern. Even though it was winter, the room was fragrant with the smell of brightly coloured flowers displayed in vases around the room.

Mr. Smith was reflected in the mirrored wall, watching Tom. Then the man tucked the sunglasses into his suit pocket and walked away. After making sure he was gone, Stephanie looked at Tom. "Okay, Mr. Detective, here's a challenge. Where's our safe hidden?"

Tom studied the room, then crossed the hardwood floor to one corner and pointed down at a small carpet. "It's under there, I'd say. There must be a trap door, with the safe directly under it."

Stephanie was staring at him. "That's amazing! How'd you know?"

"Look around the room. The other corners are bare, but this one has a carpet. There's probably something under it."

"Now that you mention it, I guess that's pretty obvious."

Tom laughed. "You sound just like my buddy, Dietmar Oban. He's the manager of our team."

"Say that name again?"

"It's pronounced Deet-mar. His name means Peter in Austrian. His Mom's from there, and his Dad's Scottish."

"What's a team manager do?"

"Looks after the equipment, keeps scoring records, that kind of thing."

"What's Dietmar look like?"

Tom smiled. "You ask more questions than I do. Oban's got black hair and eyes. He's slim, despite the amount of food he packs away daily, and he dresses really well."

"He sounds okay. I wouldn't mind meeting him."

"Maybe you will. It's a long tournament — we'll still be here after *Carnaval* ends." Tom thought for a moment. "Oban's actually lots of fun. He's always been a television addict, but lately he seems to be maturing. He's down to about three hours a day."

"What's his favourite show?"

Tom shrugged. "It beats me."

Stephanie frowned. "I've never heard of that one."

Tom laughed. "No, I meant I don't know what his favourite is."

"My mistake," she said, grinning. "Come on, I'll show you the rest of the house."

"Who's that Mr. Smith?"

"I'm not sure," Stephanie replied. "He's staying here as my father's guest. He doesn't say much."

There were many rooms in the mansion, but Tom's favourite was the kitchen. The pine cupboards and a giant refrigerator held enough supplies to fuel several parties. "My buddy Oban would love this place," he laughed as they made milkshakes with Häagen-Dazs chocolate ice cream.

A servant appeared in the doorway to tell Stephanie she was wanted on the phone. As she sat at the kitchen counter, chatting in French with a friend, Tom studied her bracelets and rings, then looked at her dark eyes and swept-back hair. She was really quite beautiful.

Hanging up the receiver, Stephanie smiled. "We've got three separate phone lines into this place, because my folks and I get so many calls."

In a book-lined study, where logs crackled in another fireplace, she showed Tom three more phones on a leather-topped desk that had a matching, high-backed leather chair. "This is my Dad's special room, but we all enjoy phoning from here. We've also got extensions in our own rooms upstairs."

Tom looked at some of the titles in the floor-to-ceiling bookshelves. "No Hardy Boys here, I guess?"

Stephanie smiled. "Mom told me about you and your sister helping the police when those bombs were discovered at the West Edmonton Mall. Are you friends with her?"

Tom nodded. "I kind of wish Liz had come on this trip. She's in French Immersion at school, so she could have translated for me."

"I wish I had a brother. Someone to talk to, you know?"

In the music room a pink chandelier glowed above the piano. "That's *Louis Quinze* style," Stephanie told Tom. She picked up a glass bowl from a side table. "This is Steuben glass, designed by James Houston. My mother bought it, but of course it's half Dad's. They share everything they own."

Tom smiled. "What a place to live. I can't wait for dinner."

"Our cook's from Paris. She gets a huge salary but Mom says it's worth it. My parents do lots of entertaining. Some really famous people have been in our house."

"Great! Who?"

As Stephanie talked about the big-name visitors they walked through the house and finally reached the dining room. The big table was polished wood, and candlelight reflected from crystal glasses and silver cutlery. Stephanie's parents were at the two ends, and Tom sat down beside her across from Mr. Smith.

A servant in a white uniform arrived with a tray from the kitchen and put bowls of soup before everyone. There were several spoons at Tom's place so he watched to see which one Stephanie's parents selected. Then he chose the same one and turned to her.

"This pea soup smells great."

Stephanie smiled. "*Potage aux pois cassés verts* is my favourite." Her big eyes looked at Tom. "We're going to the Mardi Gras banquet at the Loews Le Concorde. It's one of the world's great hotels. Mom, may Tom come as my guest?"

"Certainly."

Tom shook his head. "I'd love to, but I'm already going. My friend Michelle invited me. She's rented a really beautiful costume."

Stephanie's eyes narrowed. "Who's this Michelle?"

"She's from Baie St-Paul. Her aunt was the reporter who died."

"Oh. Right."

Commissioner Martin looked at Tom. "I understand you'll be in the parade on the hockey float. Had your computer face-scan done yet?"

He nodded. "Will you be in the security zone?"

"No. We've rented a suite at the Hilton hotel overlooking the route. It's beautiful to watch the night parade from up there."

"I can't figure what the security zone's for."

"I can answer that," Stephanie said. "You've seen the huge wall around the old part of Québec? Well, there are actually rooms inside that wall. Some *very important* people will wait inside the wall for the parade to approach, then walk to a review stand and watch it pass. The review stand is inside the security zone."

"Who are these important people?"

Stephanie looked at her mother. "May I tell Tom?"

"I suppose so," Commissioner Martin said. "You've already told him most of the secret."

Stephanie smiled at Tom. "Aren't I lucky Mom's a police commissioner? I learn all the best secrets. Anyway, Tom, waiting in that room in the wall will be the leaders of the United States and the Soviet Union. Isn't that *fantastic*?''

''They're going to watch the parade? How come?''

''I can answer that,'' the Senator said. ''They are making an important gesture to the people of Quebec City. The leaders want to share the *Carnaval* excitement, Tom, and they decided that watching the parade would be perfect. But of course it is a secret for now.''

''So we'll actually see them from our float? How terrific.'' Tom tried to picture the scene. ''Will there be any crowds watching inside the security zone?''

''Of course. But every person in the crowd will have had a computer scan. The security people are not taking any chances.''

''It's so exciting!'' Stephanie smiled at her father, and for a moment he looked happier. Then he sighed. ''You and Tom, such fine young people. You deserve a better world. That is why I applaud the presidents. Soon they will sign a simple piece of paper that says, *no more chemical weapons*. It is such an important step towards banning all weapons.''

Stephanie winked at her mother. ''Daddy's going to start his sermon again. Maybe he'll get out his old guitar and sing 'Give Peace a Chance.' ''

Commissioner Martin smiled at her husband. ''We have guests, dear. Let's not bore them.''

But the Senator didn't seem to hear. He was looking at the white drifts of snow outside the window. ''The leaders shocked the war industries of their countries when they agreed on a protocol to ban chemical weapons. They must sign the protocol.''

''Is there any chance they won't?'' Tom asked.

Senator Martin looked at him with piercing blue eyes. ''President Kennedy was killed by bullets. You think it can't happen again?''

Tom shivered, remembering the woman falling into the snow outside the telephone booth in Baie St-Paul. "Have they found that man yet? The one who drove the white car?"

Commissioner Martin shook her head. "Not so far."

"Tom," the Senator said. "Have you ever asked the government to manufacture chemical weapons?"

"No sir."

"Then why are they made?"

"I don't know."

"Because some people get a huge amount of money building weapons. Those people want to keep making money, so they convince the government the weapons are needed. Can you imagine how shocked they were, when the presidents said the building of chemical weapons must stop?"

Tom nodded.

"Some people will protect their money in any way. Now can you see the risk to the presidents? If one should die, or both, the protocol would not be signed. The weapons would continue being made." Senator Martin shook his white head. "I admit I live in an expensive house. I love beautiful things, but I also love my country. I would fight as a soldier to defend my home and family against invaders, and to defend my country. I deplore greed of any kind, including the desire of any country to swallow others. Hitler wanted to own the entire world! Because of his greed, millions and millions of people died in agony."

Tom looked at Commissioner Martin. Yellow candle-light shone on her face as she listened to her husband. It was impossible to know what she was thinking.

The senator leaned toward Tom. "In this very city, my uncle and his bride spent their honeymoon. Then she watched his troop ship sail down the river on its way to

Europe. I am sure she cried, watching that ship sail away, because her new husband was leaving and might never return. It was his duty to sail to Europe and fight Hitler's greed, and the greed of the bomb-makers who supported the Nazis.'' Again he looked out the window, thinking. ''The Nazis were defeated, but still the manufacturers produce their weapons. These days, it is even worse. Children are encouraged to want toy guns and toy soldiers with sophisticated weapons. Naturally enough, the children think that it would be wonderful fun to use real weapons when they are older. Do you see how that benefits those who manufacture such weapons?''

Tom nodded. ''Yes, sir.''

There was a long silence. Finally Tom said, ''What happened to your uncle?''

''That fine man was walking in a field close to the battle zone when a bullet came from nowhere and ended his life.''

The Senator stood up. ''I am not free of fault, myself. Pride is my undoing.'' He walked to the door, then looked at the others. ''The president and premier must not fail.''

As he left the room, Tom looked at Mr. Smith. The man had not said a word since dinner began.

7

In his room upstairs, Tom stood looking out the window.
Snow lay deep in the yards of nearby brick houses, glit-
tering where it was touched by light. Directly below his
window, Mr. Smith stood on the front porch of the Martins' house, speaking into a micro-cassette recorder. His
breath steamed in the cold air.

Tom sat down at a writing desk and made some notes.
He was staying in the Safari Room, which was filled with
souvenirs of the Martins' trip to Africa. Panthers stalked
the walls, and carved masks watched him from tables.
Using his dictionary and the phone book, Tom learned
that a tattoo parlour called *Le Tatouage* was located within
the walls of *Vieux Québec*. He noted the address, then

read over his other information. The driver of the white car was maybe called Z. Was he a hit man? If so, who was he working for?

Tom went into the *ensuite* bathroom connected to his room, loving the luxury of having it all to himself. Clear light bulbs around the mirror glowed brightly as he flossed his teeth, and water poured from a radical black faucet. Once back in his room, he flicked off the CD, the VCR and the Sony, then crawled into the huge bed. Tomorrow he'd be playing hockey in *Le Colisée* in front of thousands of people. He shuddered, hoping he wouldn't mess up, then fell into a sleep of many dreams.

* * *

Dietmar Oban stood over Tom, a wicked grin on his face. Tom groaned, wondering when the nightmare would end, then suddenly realized he was awake. It really was Dietmar Oban standing there.

"What's going on?" Tom said, rubbing his eyes.

"Are you planning to sleep forever? I just met Stephanie when I came for you, and she asked if we wanted to go cross-country skiing on the Plains of Abraham."

Tom rolled out of bed. The distant Laurentian Mountains were blue against a pink sky. "How'd the team do in the last game against Baie St-Paul?"

"It was a tie. Three-three. We might have won if you hadn't deserted us in our time of need. But seriously, how's Michelle doing? Still upset about her aunt?"

Tom nodded. "It's going to take her a while."

"I'm glad I decided to visit you this morning. Otherwise you'd probably have kept that Stephanie all to yourself."

"Got a good billet?"

"Sure, but *nothing* like yours. That's some girl, and this is some house."

"Hey, Oban, have you listened to local radio?"

"Sure. The commercials and the jingles and the chatter are just like home. I can't understand a word, but it's still fun radio, and alot of the music is the same."

Tom looked at Dietmar's ski jacket, which was the colour of jade. "Where'd you get that, Oban? It looks expensive."

"At a mall. It cost all my money. I'm wiped out, but I know I can count on you."

"Thirty percent interest, compounded twice daily." Tom pulled on his clothes. "Hey, I forgot to tell you. Before we left Winnipeg I was at a movie and everyone got up to leave."

"That bad, huh?"

"No. It was over!"

Dietmar sliced a pillow at Tom, but he was already heading down the stairs. He found Commissioner Martin in the front hall, just getting ready to leave. "*Bonne chance* with your game, Tom. I'll be hoping for Winnipeg."

"Thanks! It's nice you remembered."

"Where did your friend Michelle rent her costume for Mardi Gras? I may get something better for myself."

"In a costume shop on Rue St-Louis. You can't miss it."

"Enjoy your breakfast. I left a copy of *Mad* for you to read."

"Thanks! I'll see you later, Commissioner Martin."

Tom and Dietmar found Stephanie in the dining room, where sunlight poured through floor-to-ceiling windows. She was wearing an ivory-coloured ski suit that, she told them, came from the famous Colorado resort where she'd spent Christmas with her parents. As she described the resort to Dietmar in great detail, Tom ate breakfast and read *Mad*.

The family owned lots of ski equipment, so Tom and Dietmar had no difficulty finding boots and skis. "We can ski to the plains from here," Stephanie said as they went outside. "What a beautiful day."

Squinting against the bright sunshine they raced each other through the snowy neighbourhood and soon reached the Plains of Abraham. Other skiers were already there, enjoying the vast beauty so close to the city's busy streets.

"What's with the cannons?" Dietmar asked, looking at the old snow-topped weapons standing along the edge of the plains.

"This is where the French and English armies fought for control of Quebec City." Stephanie led them across the plains in the direction of a distant stand of trees. "We're heading toward the cliff. The English soldiers climbed it during the night. The next day, the armies fought."

"And a bunch of young guys got slaughtered," Tom said as they reached the trees. "Instead of going home to their wives and kids they died on these plains. It's what your Dad talked about, sort of."

"I don't get it."

"Well, you know. If you think about greed causing wars. Whichever country controlled Quebec City made all the money from the fur trade. So they convinced the soldiers it was important to fight each other on these plains. It seems stupid. In the end, the only people the war helped were the fur traders and the people who got rich making guns and ammunition."

Stephanie shook her head. "Mom says soldiers get paid a lot. It's a good deal for them."

"Good deal? How can you say that when. . . ."

"Hey, guys," Dietmar said. "Cut the arguing. The view's amazing from this cliff."

Under the pale sky they saw highways running past snowy farms towards the Appalachian Mountains to the south. Far below their feet, at the bottom of the cliff, were the streets of *la Basse-Ville* nestled beside the ice-filled St Lawrence River. Its white surface was broken by the path of an icebreaker, and a ferry was struggling across to Lévis.

They stayed a while longer on the plains, enjoying the perfect day, then headed back to Stephanie's house. On the way Tom paused to watch a small plow growling along the sidewalk, pushing snow aside with its steel blade. An operator sat in the tiny cab, both hands on the steering levers. "Those Bombardiers are something else," Tom said. "I could make some real money in Winnipeg clearing people's walks with one."

Back at the Martins' they made a Bonhomme in the front yard and decorated him with a toque and sash, then went inside to the pine-panelled kitchen. After drinking mugs of steaming hot chocolate they watched afternoon soaps, which Stephanie rapidly translated into flawless English, while also providing background on all the characters' stories and lives.

"I'm amazed," Dietmar said. "Your brain's faster than my computer. Ever thought of moving to Winnipeg? I need help with my French or I'm never going to pass."

As the two laughed together Tom went upstairs to get his notebook and city map. Returning to the others, he passed the study. Glancing in the door he felt his heart skip a beat. Mr. Smith stood by the fireplace, talking to himself as he stared at the blazing logs.

*   *   *

Seeing Tom, the man immediately stopped speaking. Reaching out a hand to the mantle above the fireplace, he picked up his micro-cassette and switched it off. Then, without saying a word to Tom, he walked past him and disappeared down a dark hallway.

Wishing he knew more about Mr. Smith, Tom returned to the kitchen for Dietmar. They pulled on their winter boots at the front door, then bundled up against the cold and said goodbye to Stephanie.

As they walked along streets of beautiful houses, Dietmar looked at Tom. "You don't like Stephanie much, do you?"

Tom shrugged. "She's okay. But I get tired of hearing about the logos, know what I mean? All the bragging about Colorado resorts and Polo sweats and all the expensive things they own. *Très* boring."

Dietmar laughed. "How's your French coming along?"

"Slightly better. I'm getting tired of constantly looking up words in the dictionary, so I'm forcing myself to memorize the useful ones. Like blueberry pie and ice cream."

"But not liver and onions?" Dietmar smiled. "I saw the Soviet Pee Wees play a Quebec team last night. That Coliseum is some building — it must seat sixteen thousand. They played end-to-end hockey, incredible!"

"I'm somewhat glad the tournament's broken down into different divisions. I wouldn't want to be playing against teams with that kind of strength."

Tom and Dietmar soon reached *La Grande Allée*, a busy street lined with old stone buildings that had been converted into restaurants with colourful awnings over their doors. On the roof of one building a man was knocking huge icicles to the ground, while a second worker stood guard below to make sure that they didn't hit any passersby.

"An icicle's a perfect murder weapon," Tom said. "The evidence melts before the police arrive." He glanced up at a traffic light. "Know why each colour is a different shape?"

"For colour-blind drivers. Next question."

"Why isn't that driver turning right on the red?"

"It's against the law in Quebec."

"You're on a roll today, Oban. See that fort over there? It's called the Citadel. There's only one entrance through those thick walls and they made it S-curved. Know why?"

"Nope."

"So the enemy couldn't fire a cannonball into the fort."

"Unless they used a cannon with an S-shaped barrel."

"You may have a point," Tom agreed. "Or is that just the top of your head?"

After looking at some ice sculptures they bought souvenir pins and tiny Bonhommes to wear on their jackets. Dietmar also purchased a long plastic *Carnaval* horn, which he held with both hands while producing a blast of sound. "Fantastic," he grinned. "I'll use this to wake my Dad on Sunday mornings."

The two friends walked across a vast open area where traffic rolled past, the cars forced to slow down as they approached the St. Louis Gate, one of the entrances into the walled city. Built against the wall was the Ice Palace, its packed snow a brilliant white under the sunshine. Above the ramparts, carnival flags cracked in the cold wind.

They passed through the high-arched gate in the wall and entered *Vieux Québec*. Two people in thick fur coats stood beside a *calèche*, offering rides. The carriage was open but there was a rug to keep people's knees warm, and jingle bells sounded as the horse tossed its head.

"Wow, I'd love to take Michelle for a ride!" Tom hurried over to learn the price then quickly returned, shaking his head. "Out of my league."

"Maybe I'll go with Stephanie."

"But only if she's buying, right?"

"Well, I. . . ."

Tom laughed. "Michelle's invited me to Mardi Gras. There's a seven-course dinner."

"Don't drink from the fingerbowl." Dietmar looked at a wooden platform above their heads. "That thing's just been built. I love the smell of new lumber." His eyes travelled along an enclosed walkway which connected the platform to the city wall. "I wonder what that's for?"

"See the windows of those rooms built into the city wall? Some VIPs are going to wait in a room, out of the cold, until the parade approaches. Then they'll go to the review stand."

"By the way, where are we going today? You haven't told me."

"I'm looking for a place called *Le Tatouage*."

"What's that mean?"

Tom shrugged. "Tattoo, something like that." He looked down a narrow street, where really old houses lined the sidewalks. "British cannonballs once rained down on these very streets, Oban. Imagine—we're a part of history."

"Did you just say tattoo? As in *tattoo parlour*?"

"Yeah." Tom arranged his face in an innocent expression. "Why?"

"Because I suspect you're manipulating me into another investigation. Well, listen really carefully. I refuse to visit any tattoo parlour. Absolutely refuse. Are you receiving my message?"

"Michelle's got a sister. Care to meet her?"

"I. . . ."

"We're talking major cute here, Oban. I bet she'd like that jade-green jacket you're wearing."

Dietmar sighed. "Okay, Austen, I'll go to the tattoo parlour. I can't guarantee I'll go inside."

Tom looked at his map. "We're almost there." He swallowed. "Nothing can go wrong. Trust me."

"What a hollow promise."

They began walking cautiously down a dark alley. Neither boy said a word.

8

The alley ended at a courtyard, where white twisters of
snow blew down from the roofs of surrounding buildings.
An outdoor staircase led up to a door with a sign that read
Le Tatouage.

Slowly Tom and Dietmar climbed the icy stairs, their
breath steaming in the cold air. Tom opened the door and
stepped inside. The air was thick with cigarette smoke,
making him squint and cough; displayed on the walls were
such popular tattoo designs as snakes and skulls. Behind
a shabby counter stood a man with a bony nose, and long
hair fringing a balding head. He wore a Harley-Davidson
T-shirt, dirty jeans and a leather vest.

"*Ouais! Qu'est-ce que vous voulez, les gamins?*"

"Uh. . . ." Tom went closer to the counter. His mouth was dry. "*Je le regrette mais . . .* we don't speak. . . ." He thumbed his dictionary. "*Quand. . . .*"

"Austen." Dietmar was standing in the doorway. "I don't like this idea. He looks like a middle-aged Nazi."

The man glanced at him. "I speak English."

Dietmar disappeared down the stairs. As he did, Tom looked at a big appointment calendar lying on the counter. His eyes scanned it rapidly as the man went to the door and slammed it closed.

"Was your buddy born in a barn? Heat costs money."

Tom started toward the door. "I guess we came to the wrong place."

"Why are you here, kid?"

Tom tried to look nonchalant. "I was thinking of a tattoo. You know, kind of a *Carnaval* souvenir."

The man laughed harshly. "You are not even shaving yet. Get out of here."

Soon after, Tom found Dietmar waiting at a corner. "If I'd heard screams, Austen, I'd have called the cops."

"My heart's still pounding but it was a worthwhile visit. I learned that that guy's name is Henri, from a sign on the wall, and I got a look at his appointment calendar. He's done a pencil sketch of each customer's tattoo, next to the person's name and address. Only one dagger was ordered, by someone who lives on Rue St-Laurent." Tom looked at his map. "It's not too far."

"Count me out."

"What about Michelle's sister? The deal includes your help on everything today, not just the tattoo parlour."

"Everything until three o'clock. Not beyond."

"Agreed." As they passed through the city gate, leaving the streets of *Vieux Québec*, Tom covered his ears with gloved hands. His nose tingled in the cold. "Know something interesting? The person who ordered the dagger tattoo calls himself Z. Know where else that initial appeared? In the aunt's notes.''

''So?''

''I figure Z is working for someone with a major secret to protect.''

''Who?''

''That I don't know. But I'd sure like to find out.''

* * *

Rue St-Laurent hadn't yet been plowed, but people's feet had left a rutted path between the stone houses. The telephone lines were thick with snow, and icicles sparkled in the sunshine. The street was very quiet.

''What a beautiful place,'' Tom said.

''You think Z lives here?''

''According to my map, it's the only Rue St-Laurent in Quebec City. But the numbers don't seem right.'' Tom looked at his notebook. ''I wrote down Z's address after I left the tattoo parlour. I'm sure I got it right.''

''Then let's leave.''

Tom grabbed Dietmar's arm. ''Hey, we've come all this way. Let's at least try.''

The houses were of different designs; a few had outdoor staircases leading up from the street. The boys passed some small apartment buildings, then more houses and finally a huge church rising high above.

''What are we looking for?'' Dietmar asked.

''I'm not sure. I keep hoping we'll find the number.''

''There aren't any more houses. We've reached the end of the trail.''

As they backtracked along Rue St-Laurent Tom said, ''Maybe Michelle's learned something more. She's coming to our game today.''

''With her sister?''

"Maybe." Suddenly Tom stopped, staring. "Look up there! In that window!"

"I don't see anything."

"That model car. It's exactly the same car as the white one I saw."

"So what?"

"That's an expensive car. You don't see many around, yet suddenly we spot that model in the window. It's worth investigating."

Dietmar looked at his watch. "It's three. The deal's complete. Otherwise I'd have been happy to join you."

Tom yanked back his cuff. "According to my calculations, it's only two in Winnipeg. I forgot to mention our deal runs on Central Time."

Dietmar shook his head. "One of these days, Austen. Obliteration. I promise."

Carefully they climbed the stairs. Ice crunched under their boots and the wind gusted snow along a balcony that ran past several apartments. Again Tom looked at the model car in the window, then knocked.

A woman opened the door. "*Oui?*"

Tom looked over her shoulder, hoping to spot Z, but only saw a white-bearded man in a rocker by the kitchen stove, a baby asleep in his arms. The linoleum was wet and the woman held a big scrub brush.

"*Oui?*" she said again, then tried to close the door. But Tom put his foot in the way, still searching for signs of Z. "*Veuillez enlever votre pied,*" she said, pushing Tom. Staggering backwards, he stepped on Dietmar's toe and heard him yell angrily.

Immediately the baby wailed. The woman looked at it, then at Dietmar. "*Trois heures pour l'endormir et vous ruinez tout!*" Turning, she grabbed a bucket of soapy water from the kitchen floor.

"I'm outta here, Austen!" Dietmar raced to the end of the balcony and thundered down the stairs. As he did, the woman reached the railing above his head and dumped the bucket. There was a cry from below, then Tom saw Dietmar dashing away.

Soapy water had soaked his head and his beautiful jade-green jacket.

*   *   *

Tom decided to walk to *Le Colisée*, home of the Nordiques and the Pee Wee tournament. He passed a lot of kids speaking French as they headed home from school. Signs in store windows suggested they should *Buvez Coke* or *Essayez la fantastique Friandise Mars*; lots of people wore Bonhomme pins and sashes.

Finally reaching *Le Colisée*, he found the Winnipeg dressing room. It was loud with voices calling encouragement to each other as the nervous players got ready for the game. Their coach outlined strategy on a blackboard, then they grabbed their sticks and thumped down the corridor toward the noise of a large waiting crowd.

Tom's heart was thundering as he stepped on to the enormous ice surface. The TV spotlights were powerful as he skated around the boards, gazing up at the rows and rows of seats. The turnout was amazing.

The Charlesbourg team was also on the ice, so Tom skated over to their bench, where the trainer was working on Étienne's goalie pads. They said hi to each other, then Tom spun past his team's goal to give the net a good luck whack with his stick. Moments later he was at centre ice, facing off in front of thousands of people.

Within minutes Tom knew he was in the battle of a lifetime. The Charlesbourg team was strong and fast, passing the puck with perfect timing and skill, while testing Winnipeg's excellent defence. The swift action was exciting and exhausting, but by the third period the big scoreboard still read 0 under VISITEUR and 0 under LOCAL.

By now everyone knew Étienne Ducharme was the game's first star. Time and time again he made stand-up stops at close range, several of them against Tom: early in the third period he stole a rebound in front of Étienne, with the entire goal open, but the boy's swift glove made the save out of nowhere. Even the players on the Winnipeg bench thumped the boards with their sticks at Étienne's talented stop.

Leaving the ice, Tom thought about the video he'd seen of the goalie's early career. He told Dietmar about it and then said, "You should sign the rights to that video. Étienne's going to the top."

"Most of the big names once played here as Pee Wees, Austen. But with the way you're playing today, your name won't be among them. That last shot absolutely humiliated me."

The teams continued to race the puck the length of the silver ice, over and over, but the game wasn't resolved until after a voice had boomed *dernière minute de jeu de la troisième période*. With 38 seconds showing on the clock, Tom skated swiftly behind the Charlesbourg goal with the puck and — remembering a move he'd practised over and over, coached by a superstar's video — he deeked left, then stunned himself by actually making the impossible pass, putting the puck on the stick of Jesse Silsbe at the moment he split the defence and raced alone toward the goal.

Jesse's shot was swift and perfect, giving Winnipeg the win. Later, as the two tired teams shook hands and congratulated each other, Étienne smiled at Tom. "*Félicitations*. Your move, amazing. *Je n'avais jamais vu ça.*"

Tom grinned. "You are a *très grand* goalie, Étienne. *Numéro un* — number one!"

Behind the bench waited some of the parents and family of Winnipeg players, who'd come east to watch the tournament. They were slapping backs, speaking proudly, taking photographs and videos. Jesse Silsbe called Tom over to greet his sister, Anne, who was a friend of Liz.

"She'll be furious she missed this trip to Quebec City, Tom! Dietmar told everyone about the tattoo parlour, and getting his new jacket soaked."

"I guess I was wrong about that model car in the window."

Anne studied his face. "Is it true Dietmar gets to meet Michelle's sister?"

Tom grinned. "Sure. A deal's a deal."

*　　　*　　　*

After trading pins in an echoing concrete corridor of *le Colisée*, Tom bought hot dogs and drinks and climbed into the greys, where he'd agreed to meet Michelle. Far below on the ice, teams from England and the USA were just facing off.

"Your name is in the programme, Tom. How exciting for you."

"It's great to see you, Michelle." He smiled at her. "What a game. I'm exhausted."

"It was excellent. Did you hear your name over those big speakers, when the goal and assist were announced?"

Tom nodded. "It was fantastic. I'll never forget this time in Quebec."

Michelle put her hand on Tom's. "I hope you will return, some day."

"So do I. I hope it a lot."

After a moment Michelle said, "My sister, Diane, worked again today on the computer. She has learned some important information."

"Like what?"

"Remember the word Seron in my aunt's notes? Diane has learned from the computer that it is a chemical weapon. Perhaps the Seron is being made in Baie St-Paul."

"I bet you're right! They could be manufacturing Seron at that plant called the Enclave." Tom thought about it. "Maybe the chef told your aunt about them secretly making a chemical weapon in that place. She tried to force the plant's owner to confess in an interview. Instead, she died."

"What happens now?"

"I don't know, Michelle. Today I learned the car was driven by someone called Z. . . ."

"An initial from my aunt's notes."

Tom nodded. "I was sure this guy Z lived on Rue St-Laurent. But the number didn't exist."

"There is another street with that name. Across the river in Lévis. Near the ferry dock."

"That's important information! I've been wanting to take that trip, so maybe I'll go tomorrow. Want to come with me?"

"Unhappily, I will be busy. *C'est dommage.*" She looked carefully at Tom. "Will you be okay?"

"Sure! No problem." Then Tom remembered how he'd felt, alone in the tattoo parlour. Quickly he added, "I wonder what Dietmar's doing tomorrow?"

9

BIENVENUE A BORD said a big sign, welcoming travellers aboard the ferry to Lévis. Soft snowflakes dusted down on Tom and Dietmar as they leaned over a railing, looking down at the green water. Chunks of ice drifted past, some large enough to resemble small icebergs.

"Isn't this great?" Tom said as the ferry moved away from the dock. "Don't you love travelling?"

"I just saw a programme about the Titanic so I'm not too happy about this trip, Austen. Are you certain Michelle's sister has a part-time job across the river?"

"Not exactly, but. . . ."

"Say that again?"

"I told you her sister has a part-time job. Then I suggested taking the ferry across the river. It's unfortunate you connected the two pieces of information but, hey, nobody's perfect."

Dietmar stared at the buildings of *la Basse-Ville*, rapidly shrinking as the ferry battled the river's powerful currents. On the cliff high above was the huge bulk of the Château Frontenac. "Suckered again! What's going on, Austen? Why do you need me here?"

"Ah, who knows? I just like your company."

"And I just have a nice bridge you might want to buy."

Smiling, Tom turned his face to the sun, which had appeared from behind the drifting clouds. "It seems impossible a blizzard's been forecast. This deck's so warm." As nautical flags snapped in the wind he watched the ferry plow into a thick patch of drifting ice, then looked along the deck.

"Hey, what do I see?"

Dietmar turned. Two girls were sitting on a big wooden sea-chest, eating a picnic lunch. "Things are suddenly looking better, Austen, no thanks to you." He adjusted the collar of his jade-green jacket. "I'm glad I got this cleaned."

"Going to introduce yourself?"

"Good work, *Monsieur* Detective." Dietmar quickly ran a comb through his hair, then approached the girls. "*Bonjour*! How's it going?"

They glanced up. Both had pretty faces with dark hair and eyes. When they smiled they looked like sisters.

"*Salut*," one said. "*Comment tu t'appelles?*"

"That's right," Dietmar replied. "I'm here for the hockey tournament. Winnipeg's my home, how about you? I can tell from your beautiful faces you're from Quebec. Not that girls back home aren't beautiful! But there's something about females here that I really appreciate. You like hockey? I think we'll take our division at the tournament, it should be no problem. It's been a tough struggle getting to this tournament, but gratifying. Really gratifying.''

Tom wandered over to say hello. As the girls smiled at him, Dietmar put an arm around his shoulders. "This is my buddy, Tom Austen. He's manager of our team. He gets to carry my hockey stick, and sometimes my gloves if he's having a good day."

Tom stared at Dietmar. "Wait a. . . ."

"So, what about you girls? You take this ferry often?" One of them nodded. "Every day of *Carnaval*."

"Great! Maybe I'll see you tomorrow."

"Okay. No problem."

Too soon for Dietmar the ferry reached Lévis. The captain nosed it into the dock, then let the river's swift current swing the vessel into place. Thick hawsers were thrown to workers on the dock and secured, then the passengers went ashore into the terminal.

Tom walked beside one of the girls, who cuddled a blanket-wrapped puppy in her arms. It had just been to the vet, she told Tom, but was going to be fine.

"I'm thinking of being a vet myself," Tom said. "I'll probably call my clinic *Pas de problème*."

Although the girl smiled, Tom wasn't sure if she got the joke. The puppy presented its soft head for a rub, which made him feel good, then they said their *adieux*. As the girls walked away, Tom recognized a man in the crowd leaving the terminal. He was M. Ducharme, the father of his billet in *la Basse-Ville*.

"That's Étienne's father. I stayed there first, before I was shifted to the Martins' house."

"Where you met Stephanie. Some guys have all the luck."

"I liked the Ducharmes, but their house kind of made me nervous. I could almost feel the ghosts passing me on that 152-year-old spiral staircase."

Dietmar smiled nervously. "You've got a way with words, Austen. Let's drop the ghost talk, okay? And, by the way, why are we leaving the terminal? I'm taking the next ferry back."

"What about tomorrow, Oban? Planning to ride the ferry? Hoping to see those girls again? Shall I accompany you, carrying a team picture? You look so good in your manager's jacket."

"I hate blackmail." Dietmar put his hands in his pockets. "Where are we going?"

"Michelle says there's another Rue St-Laurent on this side of the river. Maybe we can find the address where Z may live. Then we'll grab the ferry home."

"You make it sound so easy."

Rue St-Laurent ran between the river and a steep cliff heavy with evergreens. Houses here had fairly big yards; a couple of kids with snowblowers were at work, throwing plumes of white into the air.

There were railway tracks between the street and the river. Tom and Dietmar watched a freight train roll slowly past into the Lévis station. The sun had once again disappeared as a storm swirled up the St. Lawrence, winds gusting over the open water and clouds turning the sky grey. Strangely, they could clearly hear the red horns being blasted by people celebrating *Carnaval* across the river in the streets of Quebec City.

"Is that a temporary garage or something?" Dietmar was studying a polythelene structure over a car. "I guess it's for the winter, to keep from digging out after every snowstorm."

"What a great idea. We should set up a Junior Achievement company and import them into Winnipeg. We'd take the J.A. top prize for sure."

"I'll do it, but only if the government funds everything."

Tom laughed, but only for a second. Then he froze in shock. Looking in the door of another garage, he had just seen the white car.

*   *   *

The nearest building to the garage had apartments on several floors. An outside staircase led to the top apartment.

"*This is it*!" Tom exclaimed, reading the number on a mailbox attached to the outside wall beside the staircase. "This matches the address from the tattoo parlour." He looked up the stairs. They were slippery but bare of ice, so there was no risk that their feet would make a crunching noise. "Let's take a quick look."

"I've got a better idea. Let's dial 911 and let the cops deal with it."

"There's no proof of anything. How do I know Z lives here? What if I give another false alarm, like the arson emergency call I made? My reputation is already in shreds, and they'd probably lock me away."

As they climbed the stairs a car stopped in the street but Tom didn't look down at it. At the top of the stairs he stared across a snow-covered porch through a window. Inside, a man sat at a table with his back to the window. A phone to his ear, he was making notes on a pad. Smoke curled up from a cigarette. The man had a ponytail, but did he have a tattoo under his eye? Tom had to know for certain before he could call the police.

"Let's get out of here, Austen," Dietmar hissed.

Tom crept higher, packing a snowball. He tossed it against the window, then saw the man turn.

"It's him — he's got the tattoo!" Tom turned to Dietmar. "Come on, let's get out of here!"

As they scrambled down to the street someone appeared around the corner of the building, blocking the bottom of the stairs. His smile was sinister. It was Henri, the man from the tattoo parlour.

*   *   *

"Interesting timing," Henri said. "I arrived just in time to see you kids climbing. . . ."

Suddenly Dietmar slipped on the stairs and fell, tumbling down against Henri. The man staggered backwards, swearing. Tom grabbed the chance, darting down the stairs and pulling Dietmar to his feet. Then he looked up at the top apartment and saw Z appear through a door.

"Stop!" the man yelled.

Tom grabbed Dietmar's arm. "Come on, run!"

Racing down the snowy street, Tom heard the roar of a powerful engine behind them. He looked back to see Henri at the wheel of a big car. The man leaned over, opening the passenger door for Z, then the car leapt forward. Tom looked up the cliff, then over to the river. There was nowhere to hide.

*   *   *

A lone whistle sounded. A long freight train was approaching, steel wheels creaking and groaning under its weight. Three diesel engines pulled the load along the tracks that ran between the street and the river.

Tom hesitated. Using the train to escape was dangerous, but it was their only chance. He gestured at Dietmar, then they raced across a snowy open space toward the tracks. As the lead diesel approached, whistle blasting, Tom glanced back at the street. The car had screeched to a stop and the men were running across the open space, rapidly closing the distance between them.

The ground shook under the weight of the train as Tom and Dietmar ran beside the diesel. Grabbing the steel ladder that led up to the cab, Tom pulled himself onto the rungs and climbed, then watched Dietmar scramble onto the ladder. Above them in the cab, a window opened and an astonished face looked down.

"Help!" Tom yelled. "Call the cops!"

"*La police?* Okay, no problem!"

The engineer held a radio microphone to his mouth, and Tom looked back at the men. They had stopped running, and were watching the train as it rolled away. Then the men hurried back to their car and roared off at maximum RPMs.

"What a couple of creeps," Dietmar yelled. Both his arms were wrapped tightly around the steel ladder. The train rumbled and shook, blurring his face. "Believe me, Austen," he shouted, "I'd better meet Michelle's sister *really soon*. This time your investigation is beyond a joke."

*   *   *

Tom and Dietmar were soon climbing the stairs again to Z's hideout. They were now accompanied by three uniformed police officers, who took a lot of information and made many phone calls. As they did, Tom made his own notes on things that puzzled him, like some broken glass in the garbage can — a few of the bigger pieces looked like tubing, but he couldn't be sure.

"Who is this blonde woman?" one officer asked, examining some photographs. "His girlfriend?"

Tom looked at the picture. "She could be the woman I saw in the white car at Baie St-Paul."

"And you think it is the same car parked outside? Then they could be Americans, since it has a Vermont licence plate. We will learn more when the experts from headquarters examine the car."

"These magazines are interesting," another officer said, flipping through shiny photographs of guns and other weapons. "Someone has written notes beside this article on jungle tribes shooting their enemies through long tubes. They used poison darts. I bet that took some lung power."

"He is a *Carnaval* fan," said the third officer. "There are several plastic horns in this cupboard."

"I heard those across the river," Tom said. "What a noise they make." He looked down at the table where Z had been phoning. On a notepad was written FORESTS.

"I wonder what this means?"

As Tom wrote the word in his notepad, Dietmar smiled. "The Great Detective at work — I love it."

"Laugh, Oban, but that's how I got to know Michelle."

"True enough, and I *still* haven't met her sister. I'm beginning to doubt she exists."

"This evening. You can meet her this evening."

"Is that a promise?"

"Absolutely." Tom looked at his notes, thinking about Z and Henri. Then his eyes went to the frozen river and he shivered. He was certain he'd be seeing those two men again soon.

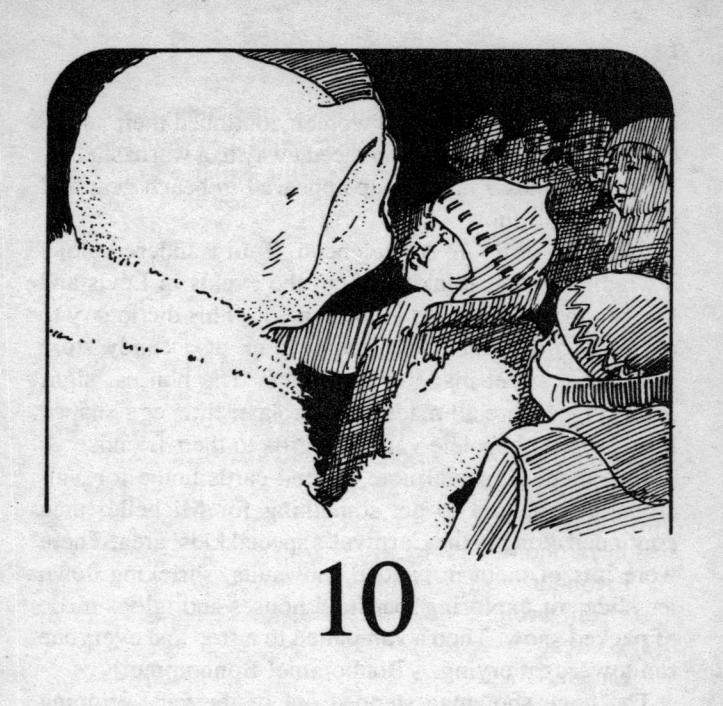

10

Snow was falling heavily in Quebec City by the time they returned. Traffic moved slowly, headlights shining against the storm. The large flakes coated people and cars, sidewalks, staircases and porches.

Tom arranged to meet Dietmar later at Michelle's house, then headed alone to the Ice Palace to watch the carnival's most bizarre event, the *Bain de Neige*. Tonight the castle was bathed in blue spotlights; people danced in front of it or blasted *Carnaval* horns, then everyone cheered as the competitors appeared.

They wore bathing suits and headbands. With loud whoops of joy they dove into piles of snow, rubbing it on their bare skin or throwing it at each other. Cheered on by the crowd, the men and women continued their snow-bath for three minutes, then raced away to a warm shelter. Within seconds a new group appeared in beach gear and dove into the snow.

When the *Bain de Neige* ended, Tom wandered along a winding street, thinking about the events in Lévis and looking in windows. At a florist he used his dictionary to place an order, then spent some time at a candy store studying a street made of chocolate. The houses, signs and bridges were all made of chocolate; little egg-shaped kids carried chocolate valentine gifts to their friends.

Tom made a mental note to send cards home for Valentine's Day, and to get something for Michelle, then continued along to the Carnival's special kids' area. There were lots of them in padded snowsuits, shrieking down ice slides or exploring toadstool houses and igloos made of packed snow. Then a van pulled to a stop and everyone ran towards it crying, "Bonhomme! Bonhomme!"

The huge snowman stepped out of the van, grinning and waving to the kids. They crowded around with shining eyes as he danced with some, then bent to talk to others. Tom couldn't follow the swift French, but he admired the actor inside the Bonhomme outfit for how easily he made the little kids laugh.

After a few minutes the van carried Bonhomme away to another event. Tom looked at his watch—Michelle was late. He took another walk around the ice houses and checked his watch again, then studied the nearby city wall. It was huge and high, thick enough to contain the rooms that Stephanie had told him about. Fascinating, but where was Michelle?

"*Bonjour*, Tom."

At last! He turned, grinning, but saw Étienne's father instead of Michelle. M. Ducharme wore a *Carnaval* toque and a Bonhomme sash. He was smiling. "Tom, how we think about you."

"Thanks, *monsieur*. How's Carrot-Fur?"

"Missing you, *je crois*. So much excitement for him when you lived up the spiral staircase."

"Please, don't remind me."

"We shall be cheering for you and Étienne in the night parade tomorrow."

"Thanks, M. Ducharme. By the way, weren't you in Lévis today?"

"*Mais oui*. I visit my uncle. You were also in Lévis?"

Tom nodded. He was about to tell M. Ducharme what had happened, then changed his mind. Instead he looked at his watch again.

"I'm supposed to be meeting a friend here. I don't know what's happened to her."

M. Ducharme smiled. "Ah, *l'amour*. It will blossom even as the snow falls." He looked at the flakes slanting down past the area's spotlights. "Such a beautiful night. Tom, I must depart. Come visit us again. *Poil-de-Carotte le veut*."

"Thanks, M. Ducharme. *Au revoir*."

*   *   *

At last she arrived, hurrying through the snow. "Tom, please forgive me! *Je suis vraiment désolée*."

"That's okay, Michelle. It's just great to see you again."

"And you. Tom, I have news of much excitement! I am late because of working with my sister at the computer. Soon she will be able to name the owner of the Enclave!"

"You mean the factory in Baie St-Paul?"

"Yes! Exciting news, *oui*? It helps me to feel less sad about losing my aunt, when we get closer to learning who was responsible."

Tom told her about finding Z's hiding place. "One thing really confuses me, Michelle. He wrote FORESTS on a notepad beside his phone, but I can't understand why. I'm sure it's important."

"*Ça me dépasse*." Michelle studied the ice sculptures, then smiled at a woman who was trying to get into a car with a bunch of balloons floating on long strings. "This is a magical place, Tom. Shall we explore for a while?"

"That's a great idea."

Passing through the St. Jean gate they entered one of the most beautiful streets of *Vieux Québec*. Lights glowed from the windows of stone buildings, shining on the people who strolled the sidewalks. Above their heads, the scene was decorated by clusters of stars and smiling Bonhomme faces. Snow drifted down past wooden signs that hung outside small shops, somehow reminding Tom of Scrooge and Tiny Tim.

There were very few *Carnaval* fans here, just local people. Students wearing berets argued politics, young couples selected apples and oranges from street vendors, and entire families crowded the aisles of bookstores, browsing. On a street corner an old man played his accordion while a girl juggled with amazing skill. They were surrounded by a crowd of people, obviously enjoying themselves.

Tom smiled at Michelle. "I love this place."

Holding hands, they wandered to the end of the street and back. Tom wanted this time to last forever, but eventually they had to leave *Vieux Québec*. After a walk of several blocks they approached the house in Rue St-Jean where Michelle was staying. A Bombardier toiled along the sidewalk, its blade clearing away the drifts, while even more snow sparkled down past the streetlights.

Tom saw Dietmar waiting outside the house. "You're sure it's okay for him to meet your sister this evening?"

"But of course. Oh goodness, *j'avais oublié*! Tom, I have exciting news. My sister has learned today from her doctor something wonderful! She will be having a baby."

"What amazing news!"

Dietmar had roses in his hand and was extremely well dressed. "I thought you'd never get here, Austen! I'm frozen."

"Sorry about that, Oban. Listen, are you sure this is important to you?"

"Of course."

Tom shrugged. "Okay."

He introduced Michelle, then they went inside. Leaving their snowboots in the hallway, Tom and Dietmar followed Michelle into a living room where a fireplace crackled. An attractive woman stood up from a sofa where she'd been reading; she was about 25, with brown eyes and a pretty smile.

Michelle turned to Dietmar. "I'd like you to meet my sister, Diane." She paused as a handsome man, about the same age, came into the room. "And this is Diane's husband, Daniel."

Tom smiled at Dietmar. "By the way, who are the flowers for?"

Dietmar stared at him in disbelief. Then, shaking his head, he handed the roses to Diane and left the room without saying a single word. Tom grinned as the outside door banged shut. "I apologize for Dietmar. He can be very moody at times."

*   *   *

Everyone separated to change into their costumes for Mardi Gras, then met back in the living room. Diane was dressed as a jockey in bright racing colours and Daniel wore a top hat and tails in white. Michelle was in the sparkling gown of a princess while Tom sported the black suit and white tie of a Chicago gangster. Beneath the fedora he wore, Tom's red hair was slicked back with grease.

Diane gave them all masks, a tradition of Mardi Gras. They were made of feathers — violet and glowing green — and completely covered their faces. While they were taking photographs the doorbell rang, and the florist came in, smiling.

"A corsage!" Michelle hugged Tom. "Oh *merci*, Tom, *merci*!"

Diane also hugged him. "And one for me! Michelle, you are fortunate indeed to meet a gentleman."

Daniel nodded. "I am impressed, Tom." He smiled at his wife. "All these flowers you are receiving! Do not forget, *je t'aime*."

She hugged him. "*Je t'adore, mon chéri*."

As they gathered their coats to leave, a beep sounded from the room Diane used as an office. "Excuse me," she said. "That should be the information on my computer search coming back by modem."

Tom waited impatiently, anxious for the results. Then his skin prickled when he heard Diane's shout of surprise.

"I don't believe this!" She came out of the office, staring at the print-out in her hand. "The owner of the Enclave is Senator Martin."

*　　　*　　　*

Soon after, Tom and the others saw Senator Martin in person, stepping from the family's limousine outside Loews Le Concorde. The huge, ultra-modern hotel glowed with lights as a crowd watched local dignitaries arriving for Mardi Gras.

Some people behind the velvet ropes flashed pictures, others just stared as the Martins swept into the hotel lobby. The Senator was in a black tuxedo but, for Mardi Gras, had worn a bow-tie of bright fluorescent colours. Commissioner Martin wore a floor-length white gown that sparkled with hundreds of circles resembling gold coins.

Stephanie wasn't with the Martins, but Mr. Smith was. He wore his three-piece grey suit and the same business shoes, not even bringing a mask for the occasion.

"At least he's not wearing his sunglasses," Tom said to Michelle. "Come on, let's go inside."

An escalator rose from the hotel lobby to the concourse level, where big cardboard houses resembled a street in New Orleans, home of the original Mardi Gras celebration. Many people in colourful costumes crowded the area, and television lights glared as cameras captured the excitement for late-night news reports. Among the reporters gathering information was Alexis Alexander, who grabbed Mr. Smith's arm and began firing questions. Tom was too far away to hear what she was asking; by the time he got closer, Mr. Smith had already disappeared into the ballroom.

Tom listened to Alexis Alexander question a man who wore a pirate's outfit until Daniel waved at him. "We are going into the ballroom!"

Tom took a final look at the reporter, then joined Michelle and the others. Inside the ballroom was a big dance floor with many round tables to each side. On the stage a band with fast hands played fiddles and guitars; they were dressed like the Beatles in their Sergeant Pepper days and had the crowd stomping along.

The *maître d'hôtel* escorted Tom and the others across the huge ballroom to a table within easy walking distance of the dance floor. The Martins were seated nearby so Tom introduced Michelle, Diane and Daniel. They briefly talked about Daniel's business, and expressed pleasure about the coming baby, then said *au revoir*; during the entire conversation Mr. Smith remained silent.

"The Senator is such a handsome man," Diane commented as they returned to their table. "How could he possibly manufacture a chemical weapon? It is *une chose horrible* to contemplate."

Tom looked at her. "What happens if the leaders sign the agreement to ban chemical weapons? Wouldn't that stop Seron from being manufactured at the Enclave?"

Diane nodded. "A lot of money could be lost."

Tom turned to Michelle. "By the way, what's happened about your parents? Are they still in Europe?"

"*Oui*. There is an airline strike. Each day we speak on the telephone. They are so unhappy, trying to get home, and not having any success."

Daniel smiled at Tom. "Do you like our snow? People in Quebec City say we have only two seasons: winter and July."

"This city's the greatest." Tom stood up. "Come on Michelle, let's have fun! Want to dance?"

"*Bien sûr.*"

They had a wonderful time dancing to the music, pausing to eat food each time more was brought to the table, then dancing again. Tom finally got tired of his mask and took it off, but Michelle kept hers, eyes grinning from behind it. As the evening continued they joined in the cheering when Bonhomme made an appearance, scrambled for balloons that fell from nets in the ceiling, and kept right on dancing as the band got steadily louder.

Later, as Michelle and Diane left the ballroom to *se poudrer le visage*, Tom approached the table where the carnival duchesses sat together. One had smiled at him earlier, so he used his painful French to invite her to dance.

As the other duchesses watched, smiling, they danced together until Tom saw Michelle's sparkling princess dress in the doorway of the ballroom. "*Excusez-moi,*" he said to the duchess. "My friend's come back from the washroom. *Merci* — that was fun."

Hurrying across the floor, Tom smiled at the brown eyes behind the feathered mask. "I missed you! Come on, let's dance."

Shaking her head, she gestured at a nearby empty table. Puzzled, Tom followed her to the table and sat down. The brown eyes stared at him for a moment, then the mask was slowly lowered. Instead of Michelle, Tom saw a young woman with blonde hair and a very tough-looking face.

"Tom Austen," she said. "If you want to see Michelle alive again, listen to me. Stop your investigation! Do you understand me? Stop meddling in serious matters or you will never see Michelle again."

11

The woman replaced her mask and stood up. "Remember what I said."

Tom stared at her in shocked silence. She looked at him for a few seconds more, then turned and began walking away, just as Commissioner Martin approached. "You promised me a dance hours ago, Tom! The music's so good."

With numb feet, he began dancing. Then he stepped away from Commissioner Martin. "I'm sorry, but my friend. . . . I've got to help her. I. . . ."

He stumbled away from her, then rushed to the concourse area outside the ballroom. It was empty of people. Then a washroom door opened and Diane came unsteadily out, leaning against the wall for support. When she got nearer, Tom saw that her eyes were unfocussed. She stumbled, and he reached a hand to support her.

"Tom!" Diane's voice was hoarse. "They have taken Michelle! I was with her in the washroom when a woman came in, wearing an identical costume. She was followed by a man, who held a gun to Michelle and led her away. The woman put on Michelle's mask, then stuck a needle in my arm. I blacked out."

"What did the man look like? A tattoo, a ponytail?"

"*Oui! C'est ça.*"

"Z!"

Just then Daniel appeared from the ballroom in search of his wife. Tom left them, raced to the escalator and plunged down the metal stairs. The lobby was filled by a party of vacationers with skis, and boots in fancy totes. Pushing through the crowd, he ran out the front door into heavy snow.

A blue van stood at the curb. The blonde woman in the sparkling princess dress was quickly getting into the driver's side of the cab. She looked back at Tom, then yelled something. Instantly the van's back doors opened and a man looked out.

It was Z. His eyes narrowed, and he jumped from the van. He was followed by Henri, the man from the tattoo parlour. Tom caught a glimpse of Michelle inside the van, hands tied and mouth taped, before Z slammed the doors closed.

The van's wheels spun for a moment in the snow before speeding away into the stormy night. As it did, Tom looked at Z and Henri. They were coming quickly toward him.

*   *   *

Tom darted across *La Grande Allée* and disappeared between some buildings. As he ran, his shoes slipped where the sidewalk had been cleared. His breathing was becoming ragged but each time he looked back the men were still following. All the houses were dark so Tom kept running, then rounded a corner and saw a garage with its door open.

Stumbling inside, he looked at the wooden beams above. There were skis on the beams, and a big piece of plywood where possibly there were boots and poles, but he didn't have time to use the skis to escape. Dropping to his knees, Tom saw just enough space to crawl under the car. Then he looked toward the street corner — the two men had reached it, and were looking for him.

Then Z pointed at the garage.

With no time to lose, Tom got into hiding and lay listening as the men approached. With tense voices they whispered questions to each other while moving around the car.

"Look under it," Z ordered.

In a moment Henri replied, "He is not there."

"Then I was wrong. That kid didn't come in here. He's escaped."

"What difference does it make? In 24 hours it will be over anyway. We will have our money and be gone. Forget the kid. You are just angry because he crossed you."

There was a pause before Z replied. "Maybe you're right. But I'd sure love to track him down."

Tom waited a long time after the men had left the garage, then dropped down from the beams where he'd hidden on the plywood. He'd found boots up there, and now put them on. Going outside with skis and some poles, he looked cautiously up and down the dark street.

There was no sign of the men. Tom put on the skis and headed down the street, still deep with snow from the storm. In the distance he saw a small Pepsi sign glowing over a neighbourhood store, but when he reached it the door was locked.

Wondering if he'd ever find help, Tom skied through the night toward a wide boulevard that was empty of traffic. Looking up at a street sign, Tom discovered he'd returned to *La Grande Allée* at the place where it ran alongside the Plains of Abraham. He looked in both directions along the boulevard only to receive a terrible shock.

A block to the west stood Z and Henri. And they'd just seen him.

*   *   *

In the distance were the twin lights of a Bombardier, working its way along the sidewalk. It was too far away for the driver to help, so Tom dug his poles into the snow and crossed *La Grand Allée* to the Plains of Abraham.

The snow was deep here, and more was coming down from the dark sky. As his skis *whooshed* across the snow Tom felt safe at last, knowing Henri and Z couldn't run through these deep drifts. Then, looking back in their direction, he cried out in dismay.

The men had hijacked the Bombardier.

The driver stood on the newly-plowed sidewalk, shaking his fist as the machine roared away with Henri at the controls. The blade was raised, and Z clung to the top of the Bombardier shouting directions.

Tom took off across the plains, driving the poles into the snow over and over again. Glancing over his shoulder, he saw the Bombardier's headlights glowing against the storm. The wind gusted snow across the windshield in blinding amounts but Henri and Z stayed on the trail left by his skis, and weren't far behind when Tom reached a stand of trees.

He'd skied past these same trees with Stephanie and Dietmar only yesterday. Tom thought of them, then again of Michelle, as he rushed down a slope. The Bombardier stayed close behind, following his trail through the trees.

Tom crouched lower as he raced toward the darkness ahead. Then he suddenly straightened up and yelled.

He was heading straight toward the cliff.

*　　　*　　　*

The Bombardier came quickly toward the scene, headlights following the trail left by Tom's skis. "Turn right," Z yelled. "Now left! That's good — we're staying with him!" Then the man suddenly looked up from watching the trail and cried out in horror. "A cliff!" Z screamed as he leapt off the machine. "Straight ahead!"

But the warning came too late for Henri. He was still at the controls when the Bombardier plunged over the side.

*　　　*　　　*

Slowly Z stood up. It was very dark now, without the Bombardier lights shining, and the man stumbled as he pushed forward through the drifts to the cliff edge.

Below him was nothing but darkness and wind-driven snow. For a moment Z stared silently. Then he turned, and disappeared into the night.

12

The next morning was cold and clear. The sun rose majestically into a pale blue sky, bringing perfect weather for the winter celebration.

Late in the day many people gathered along the riverside in *la Basse Ville* to watch the carnival's most challenging event: teams of young men and young women racing across the St. Lawrence in canoes. Equipped only with paddles, they had to fight swiftly running water and drifting ice all the way to Lévis and back.

Dietmar Oban stood watching the race from a good location. Hands in the soft pockets of his new jacket, a happy grin on his face, Dietmar smiled at the girl he'd met Friday on the ferry.

"Thought I wouldn't find you again, eh? You should have more faith!"

She smiled. "Where is your friend? The one with red hair."

Dietmar shook his head. "I'm not sure. We arranged to see this canoe race together. He was supposed to meet me at the bottom of the Breakneck Stairs." He looked at his watch. "Austen's two hours late. It's not like him."

Looking at the river, Dietmar tried to concentrate on the race. Then he saw Stephanie approaching with a group of friends. "Hey," he yelled, waving. "Over here!"

Squeezing in beside him, Stephanie and the others watched the race for a few minutes. Then Dietmar looked at her. "I'm kind of worried. Is Austen sick in bed, or something? He didn't meet me."

Stephanie hesitated for a long moment, then took a breath. "Look, something's happened." She spoke really fast. "Tom's had to, you know, go home. Back west. On a plane."

"What? He's supposed to be on the float. The parade's tonight. He'd never miss that."

"I think something's wrong at home. Back in Winnipeg, you know? That's why he went back."

Dietmar studied her large eyes. "What's the truth, Stephanie? What's going on?"

"Nothing. That's it." She looked at her friends. "Come on, this race is boring. Let's go to *La Vieille Maison du Spaghetti* and get out of the cold."

Dietmar watched them hurry away, then he looked at the girl beside him. "It's been great, but I'm leaving. Something strange is happening."

"*Au revoir, Dietmar.*"

"See you."

Dietmar hurried through the crowds jammed into streets built centuries ago. People were blasting red horns and singing and dancing together. Deciding he couldn't face climbing the Breakneck Stairs, he bought a ticket for the *Funiculaire*, an outdoor elevator that rose up the cliff. As it swiftly ascended he stood by the window, looking down at the narrow streets and the nearby river where the first canoes had reached Lévis.

There was great excitement in the streets of *Vieux Québec*. Everyone was out, singing and laughing, walking with arms around each other, and enjoying the perfect weather. Watching them were the police and soldiers who guarded the entrance to the Château Frontenac, the huge cliffside hotel where the two superpower leaders were staying. Dietmar looked up at the rooftops. There were even more guns up there, carried by sharpshooters who watched the crowd with alert faces.

Hurrying through the streets, Dietmar soon reached the St. Louis gate. The review stand was empty, but people swarmed around. Some were getting TV cameras ready; others worked on powerful lights placed along the city wall, and several set up ropes that would hold back the crowds.

"Some excitement eh, sonny?"

A man had stopped beside Dietmar as he stared at the scene. About 90 years old, his eyes were bright and alert. "I'll be here tonight," the man said. "Right inside this security zone. My daughter got special passes for me and my grandchildren. We've lived in Quebec City for years."

"I sure like your town."

"Did you hear the surprise news, sonny? It was on the radio this morning. The two presidents will be on the review stand tonight, watching the parade. Right out in the open, where we can see them. Won't that be exciting?"

"Yes, sir." Dietmar checked his watch. "Say, I'd better be going. I have to catch a bus to the university. The parade forms up there, and a friend of mine is on the Pee Wee float. I want to be sure he's okay."

Dietmar said goodbye, and passed through the wall's high-arched gate. The Ice Palace looked even more dramatic as night came to the city and the coloured spotlights were turned on. People were already gathering along the parade route. The city vibrated with excitement.

* * *

The same anticipation was in the air at the university grounds. Dietmar pushed through the crowds to the spectacular Pee Wee float, which displayed an enormous hockey stick and puck under the flags of every nation represented in the tournament.

Étienne Ducharme and the players from other countries were already on the float, but there was no sign of Tom. Not knowing what to do next, Dietmar watched a van bump across the frozen ground to a huge float that featured a jumbo top hat and oversize candles.

The driver opened the van's back doors and Bonhomme got out, waving and dancing. He climbed up on the float, then opened a small door in the base of the top hat and disappeared inside. Moments later he emerged from a trap door on top of the big hat, still grinning and waving.

"Hey Dietmar, everything okay?"

Turning, he saw the Winnipeg coach and a couple of players. "Coach! What are you doing here?"

The man shrugged. "I kind of hoped one of our guys could replace Tom on the float. It would be a major honour for the team. But I've just been told it's too late for anyone else to get a face scan done by the computer. Tom's place on the float will have to stay empty."

"But where is Austen? He was so excited about being in this parade. It kind of worries me."

The coach studied his watch. "Hey, I'm really late. I'd better get going."

"Coach! *What about Austen?*"

"I don't know anything, Dietmar. Now quit asking me."

A woman approached them. She was about 45, with intelligent eyes. She shoved a micro-cassette recorder at the coach and said, "Mind answering some questions? My name's Alexis Alexander. Your team played in Baie St-Paul, correct? I need information about that town. Did anyone there talk about a factory called the Enclave?"

As the coach answered her questions, Dietmar was taken aside by the Winnipeg players. "Hey, Oban," one whispered. "Didn't you hear the rumour? A Bombardier went over the cliff last night. Everyone's saying he was involved!"

"Who was involved?"

"Tom Austen." The boy leaned closer to Dietmar, eyes enormous. "He's gone! There's all kinds of rumours."

*   *   *

Dietmar looked at his watch. Twenty minutes until the parade would begin to move. He had to walk and think. He headed for the nearest houses, wondering what he should do about Tom. He wasn't getting straight answers from anyone, including his coach, and he was becoming really frustrated and anxious.

In the distance the night was alive with energy as the excited crowd awaited the parade. Hundreds of plastic horns were blaring, and people were cheering anything that moved, even a city truck that was spraying grit on the icy pavement. The people were stretched along a street overlooked by houses with balconies. On them, smiling grandparents looked down at the gangs of boys who paraded along the route, shouting loudly for the sheer pleasure of shouting loudly.

Next to come along the street was an elite police motorcycle drill squad that entertained the crowd by performing figure eights while everyone applauded. Kids and old folks — aunts, uncles, cousins — jammed the porches of the houses while people along the sidewalks sang and danced together. Many had red horns; the noise bounced between the walls, echoing along the route.

Then the streetlights went out, signalling that the parade was about to start.

An excited cry went up. The crowd stood on tiptoe, watching. Whistles and cheers rang out for the first marching band, which had come all the way from the state of Virginia to help celebrate *Carnaval*. Instruments gleaming, the marchers beat the air with triumphant sounds while cheerleaders high-stepped, tossing batons in the air.

The first float came out of the night. Huge, looking as big as a house, it featured Rip van Winkle with an enormous hand rising up and down in a yawn. Then came the float from the Calgary Stampede with a massive saddle that carried grinning cowgirls and cowboys, who waved to the cheering crowd.

Dietmar walked slowly along the crowded sidewalk in the same direction as the parade was moving. "This is a great event," he thought, "but what's happened to Austen?"

*   *   *

Very few of the houses in the neighbourhood of the parade route were occupied, since everyone was outside for the excitement. But beneath some roofs, people watched the parade on television because of illness.

Or for security reasons.

In one house, jointly owned by Commissioner Martin and her husband, the Senator, a television screen glowed in a darkened study where a fireplace burned. Candles cast a yellow light on the walnut walls and the big leather-topped desk, where Tom Austen sat making notes.

*   *   *

Tom swung around in the chair and gazed for long minutes into the blazing fire. Then, for the millionth time, he wrote *Where is Michelle*? and listed his facts. After that he stared again at the fire, deep in thought, and added another note: *What does FORESTS mean*?

Tom rested his hand beside the three telephones on the big desk. They were colour-coded, a pink phone for Stephanie and different colours for her parents. His fingers absent-mindedly tapped the oversized buttons of a designer phone from 2-ABC through 9-WXY as he stared at the word FORESTS.

On the glowing television screen were scenes of the parade. While glancing at the screen, waiting for the Pee Wee float to appear, Tom flipped back to his notebook pages about Z's apartment in Lévis. Why the *Carnaval* horns? Why the glass tubing? Why the magazine article on tribes killing their enemies with poison darts?

Tom looked at the screen. Every camera was focussed on the outdoor review stand where the two world leaders had just appeared. They wore heavy overcoats and scarfs, but no hats. They smiled and waved at the crowd, then lifted each other's hands in the air in the classic pose of champions.

The announcer talked excitedly about the space-age technology of the computer face-scanner that would study, from four different angles, the face of each person in the parade.

''The security's super important, folks,'' the announcer said. ''The protocol to ban chemical weapons will be signed tonight at midnight in the Château Frontenac.'' Then he suddenly exclaimed, ''Hey, Charlie! Zoom in on the *habitant*!''

The camera flashed to a man who had snowshoes strapped to his back and a strange toque on his head. Smoke curled up from a corncob pipe in his mouth.

The announcer roared with laughter. ''He's one of *ours*! Look—that fake *habitant* just pulled out a two-way radio. He's one of our government security people!''

Tom smiled. Then he stared at the screen as the picture changed to a major float featuring the huge top hat where Bonhomme danced and waved to the crowd. People were cheering excitedly and calling the big snowman's name, but Tom's eyes were horrified as he stared at him.

Bonhomme was holding a red carnival horn.

13

Tom scrambled frantically through his notes. *Red horns.
Glass tubes. Poison darts.*

He grabbed a phone to call 911. Stephanie was talking
on it in French. Hanging up, he looked at the designer
phone's big buttons reading from 2-ABC through 9-WXY.
Then he stared at the word FORESTS in his notes. A thrill
of excitement ran through him.

"That's it," he whispered. "Of course!" Quickly he
punched the 3, then 6 and the rest: F-O-R-E-S-T-S.

Tom stared at the phone as he waited for the call to go
through. Then, at last, he heard the ringing signal. As he
did, his eyes turned in amazement to the ceiling of the
room. Somewhere upstairs, a phone was ringing.

*   *   *

Tom hung up quickly, then punched in the letters one more time: F-O-R-E-S-T-S. His eyes studied the carved beams across the ceiling of the Senator's study, then his heart leapt.

Once again a phone was ringing somewhere above.

*　　　*　　　*

No longer wanting to call 911 from the house, Tom left as quietly as possible. It was cold outside, and he could see his breath drifting away in misty white clouds. He looked at the upstairs windows, trying to spot anyone watching.

The word FORESTS had been found in Z's apartment. It was a simple code to disguise the phone number of someone who was probably giving Z his orders. Calling the code made a phone ring upstairs in the Martins' house.

Tom hurried down the driveway and began running. He could hear the sounds of the parade carried on the night wind: laughter and blaring horns and the beat of brass bands. His feet slipping on snow-packed streets, Tom ran and ran until he reached the parade.

The crowds were huge, cheering for a float that carried a pirate ship with billowing sails. Tom ignored the parade as he fought a path along the sidewalk, sidestepping people and the occasional runaway dog trailing a leash. At last he saw the Pee Wee float in the distance, with Étienne and the other hockey reps waving to cheering people. Gasping for air, Tom slowly gained on it. Directly in front of the hockey reps was the Bonhomme float; it had almost reached the city gate where the security zone began.

Fireworks exploded in the sky above the Ice Palace as Tom struggled forward through the throngs of people, then was suddenly grabbed by a big police officer.

"*Tu ne peux pas aller là-bas*. That is a security zone."

"You've got to let me past," Tom shouted.

A man appeared beside them. It was M. Ducharme, Étienne's Dad. He spoke in rapid French to the officer, then looked at Tom. "This officer knows me well. I've explained the urgent need for both Canadian reps to be on the Pee Wee float. But you must still pass the computer checkpoint. Hurry!"

*   *   *

Tom rushed toward a group of security officers who surrounded a complex instrument with cameras and glowing screens. The cameras swung to Tom, the computer gave him clearance, and suddenly he was inside the security zone. Straight ahead, the Pee Wee float was slowly passing through the St. Louis gate into the walled city.

Tom ran forward, shouting Étienne's name.

"Your stick, Étienne! I need it!"

The boy looked surprised but he quickly tossed his stick to Tom, who raced forward to the next float where Bonhomme danced on top of the giant top hat. The snowman had the red horn in his hands, and was raising it to his mouth.

The two leaders were smiling at Bonhomme and waving. Behind them were grim-faced secret service agents. They were watching the crowd, watching windows, watching rooftops, but they weren't watching Bonhomme.

Tom leapt onto the float and swiftly climbed an outside ladder to the top of the big hat. Reaching Bonhomme, he raised the hockey stick and then — as the crowd cried out in horror — smashed the red horn.

Tom heard a glass tube break inside the horn, then saw the crowd surging forward toward the float. "*Bonhomme!*" they cried. "*Bonhomme vient de se faire attaquer!*"

Tom looked for the snowman but he'd swiftly disappeared down inside the top hat. He leapt forward to open the trapdoor, then found a ladder and descended to a tiny space where a door swung on its hinges.

The Bonhomme outfit had been tossed into a corner. The big head grinned at Tom as he stepped through the door in the side of the top hat. The float was completely surrounded by people crying *Bonhomme! Bonhomme!* At the distant edge of the crowd, secret service agents struggled forward, trying to reach the float. Other agents on the review stand had already swept the two world leaders away to safety.

The crowd was getting larger by the moment as Tom jumped off the float and wormed his way through the press of arms and legs. Reaching fresh air at last, he looked at the streets of *Vieux Québec*. The person who had worn the Bonhomme outfit was somewhere in those streets, trying to escape.

*   *   *

Tom slipped and slid on the packed snow as he ran from corner to corner, desperately searching the night for signs of a running man. Then, down a side street, he saw a van turning right at a red light.

"Turning on a red — that driver doesn't live here! The police think Z and his girlfriend came from Vermont!"

Frantically working his way along the icy street, Tom reached the next corner just in time to see the van turn again. It slowed, then stopped at the curb. Z immediately stepped from a hiding place in the shadows as the driver ran to hug him.

It was the blonde woman. For a moment she clung to Z, then they stepped apart and began to speak rapidly. Tom was too far away to hear so he started moving nearer, staying close to the stone walls of the houses. The night was cold and lonely.

In the distance, sirens wailed. Z and the woman looked toward the sound, then she opened the back door of the van. Tom's heart leapt when he saw Michelle inside, hands and feet tied. The woman climbed into the back beside Michelle, then Z quickly locked them inside and hurried toward the driver's door.

But he never got there.

A police car appeared at the end of the street, and another came from the west, closing in fast. Z immediately escaped down a lane and Tom raced after him, knowing Michelle would be safe within seconds.

Plunging down the shadowed lane, the man quickily reached another street. Looking over his shoulder, he saw Tom following. Darting down street after street, dashing and sliding around corners and through yards, Z tried every escape, but Tom stayed close behind. All the while, sirens cut the night above *Vieux Québec* as the police search closed in.

The man was beginning to tire. Stumbling to the end of another street, he came to a tiny park surrounded by houses and low apartment buildings. Most of the park was filled by an open ice rink. It was deserted and dark.

Suddenly the huge bell of a nearby church began to sound the hour: GONG-GONG-GONG. Other churches joined in, counting down the final seconds to midnight. As the last gong rolled across the night, car horns began sounding all over the city and the church bells rang a special salute.

Tom looked at the floodlit green roof of the Château Frontenac. Somewhere in that hotel the two leaders sat together at a table, listening to the city's joyful celebration as they signed the protocol to ban chemical weapons.

World peace had come another step closer.

*   *   *

Tom looked at the rink. He could see Z in the light coming from the nearby buildings. The man was on the ice, looking up at the Château Frontenac. Tom went forward, realizing Z had a different view of the hotel: from the rink some windows were clearly visible, glowing in the night.

Z pulled out his gun from a shoulder holster. He looked up at the hotel windows. It was an unlikely shot but not impossible. He raised the gun, selecting a window.

Tom let fly with a snowball. It sailed perfectly through the night, smashing into the man's back. He staggered, feet slipping on the ice, and turned with an angry face.

"You. . . ."

Another snowball hit the man, driving him further backwards. Swearing, Z tried to fire a shot. But he slipped again and his gun was pointed at the ice when he pulled the trigger. There was a flash of orange-red flame and a savage blast of sound, followed by the rolling echo of the gunshot. As it died away, the sound of the sirens grew louder. Z steadied the gun for a second try, looking for Tom.

"Come out of hiding, you stupid troublemaking kid!"

Tom ducked lower behind the snowbank where he was hiding.

"I said come out! Do what I say!" Z's words echoed in the cold night, his voice shrill and empty. "Do what I tell you!"

Tom heard car doors slam. He could see police officers running quickly along nearby streets. Z was surrounded.

The man put his gun on the ice. "I quit!" He raised both hands high. His skin was pale and he was trembling as his eyes swept over the approaching police. "I surrender. Just don't shoot me."

The next morning the two leaders left Quebec City. As brass bands played at the airport, their jets lifted off into the clear blue sky. Both men carried a copy of the signed protocol banning the manufacture of chemical weapons.

At the Château Frontenac, Dietmar Oban and Tom Austen arrived for a press conference in the back of a long limousine, grinning from ear to ear. They were joined on the hotel steps by Stephanie and her parents, who'd come in another limo.

Then a taxi arrived, and out stepped Michelle with her sister and brother-in-law. They were dressed up for the event, and Michelle looked terrific. Her smile was warm and her eyes shone at Tom.

Stephanie was cordial but cool when she met Michelle. Then Dietmar shook hands with Tom. "Well, so long. I've decided I'm not going to the press conference."

"Are you sure? It could be interesting."

"Nope. I'm going for a ride on the ferry."

Stephanie looked at him. "Okay if I come along, Dietmar? I suddenly don't feel very good about attending it either."

"Sure!" Dietmar smiled at her. "Both of us could probably use a friend."

Tom and Michelle said goodbye to them, then everyone went into the hotel. The lobby was fascinating and unusual. Mr. Smith left a phone booth and joined them inside the elevator. He tucked his sunglasses into his grey three-piece, then watched the changing elevator numbers with his usual steely expression. Tom noticed the man's eyes hardly ever blinked.

"I don't like heights," Commissioner Martin said. "I'm not too happy about where this press conference is being held, but the media people covering the Summit have taken all the city's other meeting places."

At last the numbers stopped changing and the doors slid open. Flash cameras began exploding in their faces and TV lights blinded them as reporters crowded around. Tom and Michelle grabbed each other's hands and hurried along the corridor behind Mr. Smith and the others. The reporters shouted lots of questions in both French and English, but one kept getting repeated:

Qui était le cerveau de l'opération?

Who was the mastermind?

*   *   *

Alexis Alexander was the most aggressive reporter. She stayed beside Tom and Michelle all the way down the long corridor, throwing question after question at them.

She was still at their side as everyone crowded into a large room where crystal chandeliers shone above, tapestries covered the walls and big windows looked down on the river. At one end of the room was a portable stage lit by television lights; Tom and the others climbed a few stairs to the stage and blinked in the harsh glare.

Mr. Smith held up a big hand to quiet the reporters. "We'll do this the Canadian way. One question at a time, and everyone else will listen politely."

A few reporters smiled at this, but Mr. Smith soon had the questioning under control. Alexis Alexander shoved her micro-cassette recorder up into Tom's face and demanded, "How'd you escape on the Plains of Abraham?"

"You mean when I was being chased by those guys with the Bombardier?"

"That's exactly what I mean. The trail of your skis went right over the edge."

"How'd you know that, Ms Alexander?"

She lifted her shoulders. "A lucky guess. I've heard a million rumours since the police tossed Z in the lockup last night. I put the likeliest rumours together into a theory. How am I doing so far?"

"Pretty good. It's true the skis went over the side, but at the last second I snapped the binders, then straightened up and grabbed a branch. I pulled myself into a tree. Once the Bombardier went over the cliff it was really dark, so Z didn't see me."

Another reporter stepped in front of Alexis. "Mr. Austen, were. . . ."

"Please, call me Tom."

She smiled. "Tom. Were you in hiding at the Martins' house?"

He nodded. "I went straight back there from the Plains of Abraham. The police figured Z might search for me, so I promised to stay indoors. A few people knew, including Stephanie and my coach, but they were sworn to secrecy.''

"What did you do all day?''

"Swam a lot of laps in the Martins' indoor pool, and tried not to worry about Michelle. Plus I worked on my notes. But the jigsaw wouldn't fit together until I remembered the glass tubes and *Carnaval* horns at Z's hideout, and realized he planned to shoot poison darts at the presidents. Which would have meant the end of the protocol.''

Alexis Alexander elbowed the other reporter aside. "This is my story, lady. Back off." She looked at Tom. "I bet Z figured he was one smart dude. He knew how to get into the security zone without a computer face-print, simply by replacing the actor inside the Bonhomme outfit. The computer cameras weren't designed to scan beneath the Bonhomme head worn by the actor.''

Commissioner Martin stepped toward the microphones. "I've been talking to some senior officers this morning. They've learned from Z that he ambushed the actor who was supposed to be Bonhomme. Z was waiting — inside the Bonhomme outfit — at the actor's apartment when the van arrived to take him to the parade. Later, of course, he abandoned the outfit inside the float.''

"What if he had succeeded with his poison dart? How could Z have escaped capture?''

"The poison would have taken about two minutes to act. Time enough for Z to shed the Bonhomme outfit and escape through the crowd. His girlfriend had arranged to meet Z, bringing Michelle as a hostage.''

"His plan almost worked.''

"You're right." Commissioner Martin turned to Tom. "My officers are very impressed with you. Congratulations.''

"Thanks!''

Mr. Smith signalled another reporter for a question. As Commissioner Martin answered the man in French, Michelle whispered a translation to Tom. "She says Z and his blonde girlfriend stole the white car in Vermont. When Z had the tattoo done, for good luck, he offered Henri much money to join the assassination plot."

"I hope the dollars bought Henri a nice plot in the cemetery."

"Listen to this, Tom!" Michelle was focussed on Commissioner Martin as she answered another question. "The police have learned why Z shot my aunt with the poison dart in Baie St-Paul."

"What's the reason?"

"The chef who worked inside the Enclave was in the plant's private dining room, listening when he was not supposed to. He learned that only part of the plant was manufacturing fertilizer. Other workers were in secret underground laboratories, making that chemical weapon called Seron. What a horrible way to earn a living!"

Tom nodded. "It's right up there with crack dealing."

"My aunt had used her contacts in Ottawa to find out who owned the Enclave. So, when she learned they were secretly making Seron, she had a hot story to tell."

Tom nodded. "Then she made a mistake, right? She should have broken the story immediately, because it was guaranteed to be headline news across the country. But she wanted the *really* big scoop and tried for an interview. She figured out the secret identity of the mastermind who was responsible for the plant making the chemical weapon, and gave that person twelve hours to agree to an interview."

"That is right," Michelle said sadly. "But twelve hours was enough time for Z to be contacted by the mastermind, told about the danger, and ordered to eliminate my aunt before she could reveal the truth about the Enclave. Then the chef's house was set on fire as revenge for what he had done. It is fortunate he is now recovering from the attack.'' She looked at Tom. ''Do you think my aunt knew about the plot against the U.S. president and the Soviet premier?''

''I doubt it. She'd have told the police for sure. Besides, there's nothing in her notebook about that conspiracy. But she was still a major danger to the mastermind, because she knew about the secret laboratories at the plant, and knew who controlled them.''

''So, Tom, who ordered my aunt's death? Who is the mastermind? That is what everyone wants to know.''

Tom nodded. ''They're about to find out.''

* * *

He turned to Senator Martin. ''Sir, may I ask you some questions?''

''Certainly, Tom.'' The man's blue eyes glanced at the reporters. He cleared his throat. ''What is it?''

''Remember talking about war when we had dinner? You really had me believing. Then I learned you owned a plant that was secretly manufacturing Seron. I felt betrayed.''

The Senator closed his eyes for a moment. ''I *am* sorry for that. But you must understand something, Tom. Every word I said at dinner was true. War is an evil thing, and we all have to work together to bring everlasting peace to our planet. Children and adults, all of us. We must never forget we share this world.''

''Then why did you make that weapon?''

''It was only last week that I learned about it, Tom.''

''I don't understand.''

''I was told the Enclave would manufacture fertilizer, so I agreed to it being built with our family's money. I am a very busy man, so I took little real interest in the plant. Then last week I decided I needed a drive in the countryside, and went out to Baie St-Paul to visit the Enclave. My arrival was not expected, so I discovered the shocking truth about the underground laboratories.''

"But you didn't do anything about them?"

"I have loyalties, Tom, as do you. And I also admit to an excess of pride. I had been tricked into having a weapon secretly manufactured in a plant that I officially owned. I faced ruin as a government senator if the truth was revealed. I needed time to think, time to make a decision."

"Well, who was in charge out there? Who was giving the orders to make the Seron? You could have just turned in that person to the authorities."

"Turn in my own wife?"

"*What!*"

The Senator looked at Commissioner Martin. "Is it not time to confess, *cherie*?" he said sadly. "Are you not the one who hired Z to prevent the protocol being signed? Are you not the one who was afraid that you'd lose all that money from making a chemical weapon? You did not care about the fertilizer—you only wanted to make Seron to kill people."

"It's for defence only," she replied.

"I do not find that reassuring." Senator Martin looked at the reporters, who were frantically scribbling in note-books and taking pictures. "Ladies and gentlemen of the press," he said. *"J'aimerais que vous essayiez de me comprendre.* I was in a terrible position. My wife had betrayed all that I believed in. Before my eyes this lovely person was transformed by greed. She wanted money, money and more money. She wanted the best house and the best cars, the best clothes and the best holidays. She taught my beautiful daughter to believe only in money. It broke my heart, and then I learned of the ultimate betrayal —her scheme to profit by making a chemical weapon."

"Everything would have worked fine," Commissioner Martin said, "except for that stupid reporter."

Alexis Alexander looked up from making notes. "Hey, that's not a nice thing to say. I worked with Marie-Claire, and she was a beautiful person. She tried so hard to make everything better for the world."

"She was a trouble maker." Commissioner Martin turned her fierce eyes to Tom. "You're one, too. I knew it the moment I met you at the police station. That's why I moved you to my house, so I could keep an eye on you."

"You gave yourself away when we first met," Tom said. "Remember when I was describing what happened at the chef's house? You got a phone call, and I stopped talking. Then you asked me about seeing the white car, and I hadn't even mentioned seeing it in the woods." He paused. "Right after that, you gave me your private phone number. Z had the same number written down in his hideout, except in the code word FORESTS."

"Z was a fool," Commissioner Martin said bitterly.

"Last night, watching the parade on TV, I realized the truth about the conspiracy against the presidents. I picked up the phone to call police headquarters, then looked at the dial and understood the code word. I called FORESTS and heard a phone ring upstairs. That's when I knew the mastermind was someone in the house." Tom looked at Mr. Smith. "I knew you weren't the one, because you have the same handshake as my parents. It's the special handshake of an organization of important people who work secretly for peace. Isn't that true, sir?"

"That's right, Tom. I'm with the government in Ottawa. I've been staying at the Senator's house while I get his ideas on how we can achieve peace. It was really thought-provoking stuff. Once or twice you saw me around the house, dictating ideas into my micro-cassette."

"So," Tom continued, "the mastermind wasn't Mr. Smith, and I doubted it was Stephanie, so who did that leave in the house with a personal phone line? Senator Martin, and Commissioner Martin." He looked at them both. "One of you learned from me the location of the shop where Michelle rented her costume for Mardi Gras, then conveniently asked for a dance just after the blonde woman replaced Michelle to give me that warning." He turned to face Commissioner Martin. "I guess you were giving her a chance to escape from the hotel. Too bad it didn't work. Too bad you'll be going to prison now."

"Not a chance!"

Commissioner Martin ran swiftly to a door marked SORTIE DE SECOURS — FIRE EXIT and disappeared through it. Tom and Michelle were the first to react; they raced to the door and discovered an inside staircase with metal walls and iron steps. Commissioner Martin's feet sounded from above, then they saw her escape through another door.

Tom and Michelle took the stairs two at a time and discovered a long, narrow hallway with doors on both sides. It looked deserted. The only light came through the window of a distant outside door.

Commissioner Martin was running toward the door. Tom and Michelle went after her, their swift feet echoing in the hallway. Commissioner Martin was looking back at them over her shoulder, not seeing a sign on the door that warned DANGER! SORTIE DE SECOURS SEULEMENT — EMERGENCY EXIT ONLY.

"*Watch out*," Tom yelled. "The door! It's. . . ."

Still running, Commissioner Martin knocked the door open and plunged outside onto a small, flat roof. Her feet skidding on the snow, she tumbled toward a low wall at the roof edge.

"*Non*," Michelle cried. "*Non!*"

Commissioner Martin almost went over the side but at the last second she was able to grab the wall, and desperately clung to it. Far below were the snowy streets of *Vieux Québec*.

"Help me," Commissioner Martin begged. "*Aidez-moi!*"

Racing forward, Tom and Michelle managed to grab the woman's arms. With a great effort they helped her struggle back to safety, just as other people arrived to help.

For a moment Commissioner Martin lay on the roof, gasping. Then she whispered, "You saved my life. Thank you."

Michelle looked down at her. "I loved my aunt. I cry for her every night. She died because of your greed."

People helped Commissioner Martin to her feet. She brushed feebly at the snow on her clothes, then was led silently away.

Tom and Michelle were alone at last. The roof was windy and very cold. Smiling, they put their arms around each other. "By the way," Tom said. "Happy Valentine's Day." He took a deep breath. "Michelle, I. . . ."

"*Oui?*"

"I. . . ." He looked into her brown eyes. "Michelle, *je vous aime*."

She held him tighter, then put a soft finger on his lips. "*Non*, Tom," she whispered. "In Quebec we say *je t'aime*."

When Eric Wilson began writing books he had two
simple goals: to excite kids about reading while telling
thrilling stories that take place in Canada. His books are
now enjoyed by readers in many different countries
around the world.

Asked the secret of creating suspense, Eric replies,
"First, make your reader desperate to know something
such as who's behind a conspiracy, or why attacks are
being made. Then, don't tell your reader the answer for
a long time!"

Eric also suggests that if you are a young writer, then
you should make use of events that have actually
happened to you, and have stories take place in settings
that you can describe accurately, such as your own
school or neighbourhood.

Have you joined

THE ERIC WILSON MYSTERY CLUB

????

It's exciting, and it's all FREE!

Here's what you'll receive:
~ a membership card
~ a regular newsletter
~ a chance to win books
personally autographed by
Eric Wilson

It's FREE, so just send your name, date of birth,
home address with town and postal code to:

The Eric Wilson Mystery Club
Harper & Collins Publishers Ltd.
Suite 2900, Hazelton Lanes
55 Avenue Road
Toronto, Ontario
M5R 3L2

VANCOUVER NIGHTMARE
A Tom Austen Mystery

Eric Wilson

Tom's body was shaking. Spider could return at any moment, and there was still a closet to search. Was it worth the risk? He hesitated, picturing Spider bursting through the door with rage on his face.

A chance meeting with a drug pusher named Spider takes Tom Austen into the grim streets of Vancouver's Skid Road, where he poses as a runaway while searching for information to help the police smash a gang which is cynically hooking young kids on drugs.

Suddenly unmasked as a police agent, Tom is trapped in the nightmarish underworld of Vancouver as the gang closes in, determined to get rid of the young meddler at any cost.

THE GHOST OF
LUNENBURG MANOR
A Tom Austen Mystery

Eric Wilson

"Would you like to visit a haunted house?"

With this invitation from a man named Professor
Zinck, Tom Austen and his sister Liz are swept
up in spine-chilling events that will baffle you,
and grip you in suspense.

A fire burning on the sea, icy fingers in the
night, an Irish Setter that suddenly won't go
near its master's bedroom, a host of strange
characters with names like Black Dog,
Henneyberry and Roger Eliot-Stanton, these are
the ingredients of a mystery that challenges you
to enter the ancient hallways of Lunenburg
Manor, *if you dare*.

DISNEYLAND HOSTAGE
A Liz Austen Mystery

Eric Wilson

Renfield held a wriggling, hairy tarantula in his hand. Suddenly the maniac cackled, and ran straight at me with the giant spider!

Facing a tarantula is just one of the exciting, suspenseful moments that Liz Austen experiences in DISNEYLAND HOSTAGE. On her own during a California holiday, unable to seek the help of her brother Tom, she is plunged into the middle of an international plot when a boy named Ramón disappears from his room at the Disneyland Hotel. Has Ramón been taken hostage? Before Liz can answer that question, her own safety is threatened when terrorists strike at the most unlikely possible target: Disneyland itself.

THE KOOTENAY KIDNAPPER
A Tom Austen Mystery

Eric Wilson

*Only groans and creaks sounded from the old
building as it waited for Tom to discover its
secret. With a rapidly-beating heart, he
approached the staircase*

What is the secret lurking in the ruins of the
lonely ghost town in the mountains of British
Columbia? Solving this mystery is only one of the
challenges facing Tom Austen after he arrives in
B.C. with his sidekick, Dietmar Oban, and learns
that a young girl has disappeared without a
trace. Then a boy is kidnapped, and electrifying
events quickly carry Tom to a breathtaking cli-
max deep underground in Cody Caves, where it
is forever night

VAMPIRES OF OTTAWA
A Liz Austen Mystery

Eric Wilson

*Suddenly the vampire rose up from behind a
tombstone and fled, looking like an enormous
bat with his black cape streaming behind in the
moonlight.*

Within the walls of a gloomy estate known as
Blackwater, Liz Austen discovers the strange
world of Baron Nicolai Zaba, a man who lives in
constant fear. What is the secret of the ancient
chapel's underground vault? Why are the words
In Evil Memory scrawled on a wall? Who secretly
threatens the Baron? All the answers lie within
these pages but be warned: *reading this book
will make your blood run cold.*

SPIRIT IN THE RAINFOREST
A Tom and Liz Austen Mystery

Eric Wilson

The branches trembled, then something slipped away into the darkness of the forest. "That was Mosquito Joe!" Tom exclaimed
  ."Or his spirit," Liz said. "Let's get out of here."

The rainforest of British Columbia holds many secrets, but none stranger than those of Nearby Island. After hair-raising events during a Pacific storm, Tom and Liz Austen seek answers among the island's looming trees. Alarmed by the ghostly shape of the hermit Mosquito Joe, they look for shelter in a deserted school in the rainforest. Then, in the night, Tom and Liz hear a girl's voice crying *Beware! Beware!*

THE GREEN GABLES DETECTIVES
A Liz Austen Mystery

Eric Wilson

I almost expected to see Anne signalling to Diana from her bedroom window as we climbed the slope towards Green Gables, then Makiko grabbed my arm. "Danger!"

Staring at the house, I saw a dim shape slip around a corner into hiding. "Who's there?" I called. "We see you!"

While visiting the famous farmhouse known as Green Gables, Liz Austen and her friends are swept up in baffling events that lead from an ancient cemetery to a haunted church, and then a heart-stopping showdown in a deserted lighthouse as fog swirls across Prince Edward Island. Be prepared for eerie events and unbearable suspense as you join the Green Gables detectives for a thrilling adventure.

CODE RED AT THE SUPERMALL
A Tom and Liz Austen Mystery

Eric Wilson

They swam past gently-moving strands of sea-weed and pieces of jagged coral, then Tom almost choked in horror. A shark was coming straight at him, ready to strike.

Have you ever visited a shopping mall that has sharks and piranhas, a triple-loop rollercoaster, 22 waterslides, an Ice Palace, submarines, 828 stores, and a major mystery to solve? Soon after Tom and Liz Austen arrive at the West Edmonton Mall a bomber strikes and they must follow a trail that leads through the fabled spendours of the supermall to hidden danger.

SUMMER OF DISCOVERY

Eric Wilson

Rico's teeth were chattering so loudly that everyone could hear. Ian's breath came in deep gasps. A gust of wind slammed through the old building, shaking it so hard that every shutter rattled, and then they heard the terrible sound.

Somewhere upstairs, a voice was sobbing.

Do ghosts of hymn-singing children haunt a cluster of abandoned buildings on the Saskatchewan prairie? The story of how the kids from Terry Fox Cabin answer that question will thrill you from page one of this exciting book. Eric Wilson, author of many fast-moving mysteries, presents here a tale of adventure, humour and the triumph of the human spirit. It's an experience you'll never forget.

THE UNMASKING OF 'KSAN

Eric Wilson

Looking back, I saw Bear near the doorway .I knew he'd never stop chasing us while Dawn had the raven mask. "Get rid of that thing!"
"Not a chance," she said. "Come on, run faster."

The theft of a valuable mask brings sorrow to Dawn's people. Determined to recover it, she turns to Graham for help and together they begin a search that plunges them into suspense and danger. The rugged mountains and surging rivers of northern British Columbia are the backdrop to an adventure you will never forget.

THE
ERIC WILSON
BOXED SET

Containing four paperback editions of some of
Tom and Liz Austen's best mysteries:

MURDER ON THE CANADIAN
VANCOUVER NIGHTMARE
THE GHOST OF LUNENBURG MANOR
DISNEYLAND HOSTAGE

Now available in bookstores everywhere!